THE GENERALS OF DEATH

THE BEGINNING OF THE END

RITVIK GUPTA

ISBN 979-8-88805-449-9

CHAPTER 1

"Hey there. What are you doing pal? Can you hear me? The voice was distant and blurry. Familiar but blurry. But who was it?

"Are you alright? You were out for hours. Do you need something?"

My eyes started to open, but it was still not clear. I could barely make out a buff dude, all bothered and bleeding.

"W…Water." I barely let that out. The man poured a few drops of water on my dry lips, but it felt like I had a few gallons. It felt like I had water for the first time. Oh! So delicious.

B…But who is the man, why was I knocked out, and what's he doing here? I had too many questions popping up in my mind, and none of those were accompanied by any answers. It might have been too much for me because I passed out.

"Hey…Hey Dude, what happened?"

There was that voice again. I was feeling an "inch-worth" better.

I reckoned I could stand up again, something which looked like a mighty task the last time I woke up.

"Wh…re…u? was all that came out. I was still very weak and helpless. I tried to blurt out something else, when the man said, "It's all right. Just rest. It's been a rough couple of days."

So, I've known this man for a couple of days atleast. But I had no idea, which corner this rat belonged to, metaphorically speaking.

After drifting between consciousness and unconsciousness for what felt like a whole lifetime and ten seconds, at the same time, I was feeling a whole lot better. I sat up, finding the man sitting nearby on a chair looking at me with contentment.

"Do I know you?" I asked with curiousness.

"Yeah, sure! If you wanna say that." That was quite vague, I thought to myself.

With all the energy I could gather, I tried scanning my surroundings.

I found myself looking at almost nothingness. Tattered up walls, moldy, with blood stains here and there. A couple of broken boxes and clothes complemented the environment, what I would describe as, post-apocalyptic.

Contrary to this, the view, as could be seen from the many broken windows, was calming and subtle. It was barely morning, and the grey clouds were allowing tidbits of the sun rays to sprout. It looked like it would pour, and I found it calming.

Among all this commotion, my alleged acquaintance had found his seat near to where I was laying.

"Anyways, however, are you my friend", he asked rather dauntingly.

"Could be better, I guess." I was rather surprised at the ascendance of my speaking ability, "Tell me… What is all this, an…and what happened to me?"

"Ohh," he chuckled. "These are some damn hard questions dude… answers to which I have! But you'll have to buckle up. This may take a while."

I could see a faint smile on his face and something else… like excitement, but not exactly.

Looking back on my inability to move, I said, "Well, it doesn't look like I'll be doing much of anything any soon."

"Hmmm… that seems likely… Well then, no better time than now!"

He adjusted himself to a more comfortable position and started excitedly.

"To make you understand everything, allow me to take you back… 6 years. The day it all began…"

"The weather's great today, Eddie. It's a perfect day for a trip uptown."

"Nahhh man. I don't feel like it. I think it's about to rain."

"Well, that's where all the fun is. I fancy this weather. It's really calming."

"Sorry, Ray. I have to pass. I don't feel up to it."

"Oh my God. You are such a spoilsport… Well, never mind."

These two young gentlemen are what you call "prodigies". And what are these two gents doing here? Well, they just completed official training for a legal license for "bomb disposal", and are currently chilling with a few colleagues in the beautiful city of Venice.

Just about 20 minutes after the usually-active Eddie's dismal traveling uptown, the boys heard something they least expected.

There was a deafening blast somewhere nearby and its shockwaves were quite absurd.

Eddie shouted, "Holyyy shit! What just happened? This was too damn loud."

"Yeah, you're right. We should go and check it out. This is not something normal," nodded Ray.

"Bro, are you guys thinking of going there?" It was Ollie, one of their comrades who had just entered the room. "There might be more of 'em coming though."

"We cannot just sit here with our hands crossed, dude. We are well equipped with knowledge. No need to hold back," said Eddie.

"Anway, I think we should go and investigate," stated Ray with authority.

Bagged and suited up, these three along with two others, George and Cain, set out to uncover the mysteries of what they penned, "The Big Blast Of Venice".

After about an hour of silence and muddled up thoughts, the five of them reached the epicenter of the explosion, a sight no one would believe was a peaceful city mere hours ago. The ground, engulfed in thick black smoke, was now home to hundreds of crushed and charred bodies. It was truly a gruesome sight to witness.

With nothing left of the place for a kilometer-wide radius, there was nothing that could further any hypothesis that the young'uns had. All they had right now were questions and anger.

Anger was definitely clouding their ability to rationalize, especially Eddie, given his short temper. But, this wasn't the case with Ray. He was calm and collected. He put his brain into second gear, analyzing all possibilities of the explosive's origin.

He laid out his thoughts. "Whatever this was, it was too large to have been done by an ordinary group of terrorists. I can only conclude it was some sort of secret government employment, but that is just speculation at this point…"

"No government would be in their right mind to something like this in the MIDDLE OF THE CITY," Eddie interrupted, clearly pissed.

"Which is why," Ray continued, "I think this might be something much worse. A group, so large it had enough expertise, manpower, and materials to plot such a thing."

"If Ray's hypothesis is even half correct; if there is such a gang, we will have to make haste," said George.

"Indeed. We must not be too reluctant," they all agreed.

Acquiring this new resolve, they all set to gather more resources to uncover the truth about this adversity. They tried to contact the few sources they had, being new in the industry, for any nick and knack of information.

Amidst all this, Eddie laid out a suggestion, which was hard for all to digest.

"This detonation might have been developed using some sort of concoction of 'azidoazide azide'."

"What? Isn't it the most powerful explosive compound in the world?" George said shockingly. The color vanished from all the faces.

"But it is impossible to buy such a large amount of the compound… Wait! This means my intuition might be on point with the large underground society." Ray concluded

"I am just saying this is a possibility. It might all be wrong, dudes." Edit try to cheer them all up but in vain. Even a slight chance of this rumor being true was disastrous news for all.

Just when all of them were fighting with the silence, the ice broke when they got a call that there had been two other simultaneous blasts.

"What?... Where?... In Italy, you say… where in Italy?... Sanremo… Uh… in the Liguria region… Ok, ok. We're heading there asap."

Without any further inquiries or words, they boarded their vehicles and rushed to Sanremo, which had allegedly experienced twoblasts in a single day.

In the six-hour journey they made, everyone was anxiety-stricken. Never before had they thought of experiencing such absurd feats, even before their careers had properly sprouted.

"Sanremo is an odd place to attack. It's not that big of a place, is it?" George tried to break the ice.

"No. it is not. But, what it is famous for is explosives, it just might be the perfect place here in Italy to trade in bombs. And, allegedly the government has less rein over its governance, so it would not be a surprise to encounter the old chap, 'illegal and underground society. And God knows what is sold under the table to who all." Eddie sounded taken aback while he replied.

Ray had never seen Eddie this tense. Although, understandably they had never experienced a situation this grave before, that too up close.

After the most restless six hours of their lives, they arrived into pure chaos. The site was considerably worse than Venice. The explosion was terrible. It created a huge crater in the center of the city, right where it blew up. And apparently, the place had been a sort of mart selling various bombs.

"Oh, Christ! There is nothing left of this place." Eddie exclaimed horror-struck.

Moving on, they went to the second scene of the incident, which was a train blast.

The survivor count was a big zero. Due to more than half the city being blown up, there was no police force to be seen. They carefully examined the hell they had just transcended into. Bodies stretched till oblivion, and there were crimson black flames all around signifying the fuzziness of the situation. It was as if the dead were rising before their eyes. This was truehell.

This was a situation beyond words. All five of them tried scavenging for any clue, but in vain, until they heard a deep rugged voice from behind. They were startled.

"Fancy seeing you lot here…Well, let's not say fancy, shall we?"

Who was this degenerate fellow? READ THE ROOM DUDE.

"WHO IS IT?" shouted Eddie, clearly furious. "…Wait…what? What are you doing here?"

"Bu…But you…died. How is this possible?" George was dumbfounded and so were the others.

A big bulky bloke with a huge scar occupying the majority of his face was standingthere with a smug look on his face. He was rough looking, about 6'2", and wore numerous other scars as proud "spoils of war".

"Brat no. 3, Georgie huh! Would it have been like me to not have cheated inevitable death? Hahaha." He had a voice deeper than the pacific with a hint of a British accent.

The five were too bewildered to say anything.

"For now, let's keep all this aside and try to make something out of this situation we got on our hands," Ollie spoke.

"You're right bro. We got bigger fish to fry. Let's worry about the old geezer later," Eddie chuckled.

"Oi, brat. Don't try to sink your head too deep… Anyway, you're right. This here is the biggest and crispiest fish in the market right now, no pun intended." He reciprocated Eddie's laughter but was smugger.

"So, how did the first bite that you took taste, former captain BLAZER?" Ray said in a taunting manner.

"Take a look at the smart bloke eh! You're as sharp as ever Ray." Blazer smiled with a cigarette now caressing his large mouth. "Well anyway, you are right. I am not here for sightseeing, believe it or not. I have a few rounds up my sleeve."

"That's what we like to hear, man. Hahaha," exclaimed Eddie as though he forgot about where he stood just then.

"NOVA," said Blazer.

"Huh?"

"NOVA is the one we're looking for here. That is the biggest underground society you could imagine. With unfathomable manpower and a lot of geniuses in the mix, they are sitting above most national armies right now. Truly mind-boggling!" explained Blazer.

"Interesting." Eddie went deep into thought. "Very interesting!" He was on the brink of jumping with excitement.

"Hmmm. Eddie boy, pipe down, lad. You might be some of the best guys for the job given your "John Wick"ing ability and extensive knowledge of the explosive industry, but trust me, this is a taste even your palate doesn't identify. Blazer suddenly turned serious.

Cain finally spoke, his all-serious look now turned into a maniacal smile.

"We'll see about that."

CHAPTER 2

My vision was fuzzy again. I must have passed out again. Was that all a dream? The five? Blazer? NOVA? Blasts?

My head started to hurt.

"Here, dude. Have a glass of water."

I looked up to find that man from before. Oh! Yeah, right! That wasn't a dream. It was the story he was narrating.

I tried to move. Huh! I had somehow reverted to how I was before. That spark of relief of being able to move had vanished.

"So, tell me, bro, did you enjoy the story? It's stimulating innit?"

"S…Sure, I guess." I wasn't sure how to respond to that.

I dumped down the glass of water and felt the same godliness I felt before.

"Sorry to doze off back then. Let's continue if you don't mind." I had a few more drops of energy in me now.

"Yeahhhh, be my guest, dude."

It had been exactly three months since the blasts in Italy. The five and Blazer teamed up to dig down on the situation. But all they were able to find was one location. A facility in Russia.

"Three months of bashing our heads together and all we have is one location." Eddie was frustrated.

"And I don't think we would find anything substantial there anyway, since we were able to discover it and nothing else," remarked George.

"Yeah, you may be right. But, this is our only lead, so we got no choice," Ollie nodded.

However, Ray was skeptical.

"Who was it that concluded activity in Russia?"

"I believe it was Eddie," replied Cain.

"Nah… wasn't me dude. I was told by Blazer. I just transferred the message… Why do you ask Ray?" asked Eddie.

"Blazer, Huh?" Ray took a short pause but kept his thoughts to himself. "Uh…nothing…nothing at all… Where is that geezer anyway?"

"He's gathering together some resources for our departure to St Petersburg," George confirmed.

"Ohh! Someone's enthusiastic," Eddie chuckled.

After a whopping eleven or so hours of travel, the six of them landed in Saint Petersburg call mom all suited up, showing off a business look.

Their ultimate destination was "Buynaksk" which had a significant history of bombings.

The headline of the information was a truckload of explosive manufacturing materials spotted moving into a tiny house, which was not much to go on, but these sixwere nothing short of being adventurous.

"We have to be careful. This might very well be a trap or it just might be a stupidly oversized school project." This sure seems like a joke but Ray's face said otherwise. He was dead serious.

For obvious reasons, they gave up their MIB look and changed into more blending clothes but were still equipped with all the techy stuff that blazer was able to secure given his military influence.

"So these were his preparations, huh!" Eddie seemed to be in a lighter mood but he was fully focused, given the ambiguous nature of their mission.

The core objective of their plan today was to just scout out the facility find the confirmation of a Nova camp and gather information. That is why George and Ollie stayed in a rented jeep for an emergency escape, just in case. And Cain stayed on standby near the alleged facility in a small open restaurant just to steer clear of any shady characters that might be approaching.

It was just Eddie and Ray accompanied by Blazer despite Ray's reluctance in taking him, given his abnormal size.

The trio entered into what looked like a small storage house, all dusty and weary. There seemed to be no guards or any sort of surveillance, looking from the surface.

Surprisingly enough, there was not a single soul in the house. Their sole companion was the creaky silence along with the webby furniture. They treaded further to discover a shady staircase moving downwards. Oh! The classic basement trope.

As they slowly but cautiously followed the stairs, the creaks from their footsteps filled the emptiness of the house.

That's when they saw a bulb suddenly pop up towards the end of the small hallway they had stepped into.

A sole man with a fresh cigarette in his mouth sat across a trapdoor, newspaper in hand. He seemed to be solving crosswords in Russian.

As the three of them moved towards him, he kept the newspaper aside and lighted his cigarette. The whoosh of the match echoed through the room.

"What you need?" he asked in Russian, with a very deep and scratchy voice, almost like his voice box was swollen.

Eddie replied, in Russian as well, "We come here to work. First day."

"Show ID."

Now thanks to a "Blazer-miracle", they had three fake IDs of NOVA workers who were supposed to be immigrating into Russia to work there. The origin of those IDs was still a mystery and how was Blazer able to make identical ones in the first place was an even bigger one.

The guy thoroughly examined them and felt satisfied with their genuineness.

He went to carefully check the three for any weapons but thanks to the 2040 nanotechnology, his efforts were in vain.

"Let's go."

He opened the trapdoor to reveal a dark staircase leading into oblivion. Picking up an oil lamp from nearby, he began his descent and they followed keeping their distance.

They soon entered, what looked like storage for grains and stuff, but was currently host to numerous empty boxes and crates along with some filled ones. There were only leftover and fallen seeds from previous stocks.

There was complete pin drop silence, except for the slight intentional rustling of their footsteps.

The Russian guy went straight towards a pile of boxes placed in a random place in the room. Neither towards the corner nor in the complete center. Among the numerous piles, nothing special made that particular pile stand out. Probably to hide whatever it was concealing in plain sight.

He moved aside the boxes there which were quite heavy. Despite having a weak build, he was moving them with ease.

And there beneath them was a fully metalled trapdoor with a display screen demanding a footprint scan. They all had to step on it for identification and verification purposes.

This was another thing they feared. Infiltrating the facility was one thing, but how to infiltrate into their database as genuine workers? On top of that, they didn't know shit about NOVA.

Cutting back a month, this topic had come up during their discussion. It was Ray who put forward the empty bowl.

"Well, we would have to do something about verification. I don't reckon, a terrorist group this hard to crack open would just let three people enter their secret facility just for having some cards."

"Oi, brat! Who do you think I am, huh? Leave this to daddy eh." Blazer smiled proudly.

"Are you sure? This ain't going to be a walk in the park," said Ollie.

"Ollie bro. Let's see what the old guy can do," Eddie laughed.

Blazer was up for the challenge. Ray looked dissatisfied but put the thought at the back of his mind.

Coming back to the present, to Ray's surprise, the verification worked smoothly. As the metallic doors of the trapdoor slowly retracted to the sides, they revealed a well-lit futuristic-looking pipe. One which you would probably slide through.

The Russian guy first ordered Eddie to go through. As he sat down and put his feet inside it to slide through, he got sucked into it.

Next was Blazer. The hole would clearly not fit the massive truck.

He shouted at the dude, "Oye blud, this ain't gonna fit me?"

The guy replied in Russian, "Keep your mouth close and step into it."

Blazer did as he was told. As he put his legs forward, the mouth of the pipe expanded to perfectly fit Blazer.

Ray jokingly said to the guard, "Just what you would expect from NOVA."

"Shut up. Don't say the name outside. Get in." He clearly wasn't trying to be friendly.

They all slide into the pipeline which seemed to go on for forever. After an eternity of sliding, they entered into something that blasted their minds off. It was a full-scale factory. Probably even larger than the average production mill you would find.

There was a huge doughnut-shaped workstation in the centerand it stretched upwards into the sky-high ceiling and about 10 more lanes extended from its sides into the surrounding walls. This place was so outrageous, and it was probably equipped with technology not yet known to the outside world. And, there were countless workers all indulged in various things, which largely included carrying around and sorting weaponry.

On this note, the 5 and Blazer's first part of the mission was a success. Now for the tricky part. They had to try and dig up information on the NOVA and escape successfully without raising suspicion.

The guard left as soon as they got there. And almost as quickly, another guy who looked like he was a supervisor came toward them.

He was dark-skinned, tall, and had huge ray-bans on, even indoors. He said, "New Americans, huh?" His English was not the best, given his heavy Russian accent. "Here, take this and get to work. Chop Chop."

He went on to explain to each of them their work and luckily each of the three wasto work in separate departments. This way they could have a more efficient newshunt and keep the search more widespread than whilst sticking together. This was perfect.

They thanked the dude, who was apparently a senior worker, which was just someone who was working fora long time.

"So there are no positions of authorityhere? Or are they purposely holding back something? What was going on here?" Ray thought to himself. "There should be no way they are suspicious of us."

The three split up and went into their respective tunnels to go on and work relentlessly without any breaks.

It had been seven hours. Given their physical prowess, none of them even broke a sweat, but for the sake of normality, they put forward a gig of breathlessness and dehydration…just to blend in.

During the long hours, Eddie found out from a random Mexican dude that this facility was just a minor armory amidst an ocean of others, and that there was only a supervising manager but he rarely showed himself.

But Ray hit bingo when he overheard two Jamaican dudes chatting about the difference between the conditions here and the colossal facility in Arizona and how it provided much better conditions. This was it! They had their next lead. Their mission definitely did not go down in vain.

According to protocol, they were supposed to gather in special dormitories allotted to them. But the three after meeting up slipped past the herd and headed to a fire exit that Blazer had spotted. They were able to trace their way to the ground without any complications.

But… just before reaching the top, they saw the exit being guarded by two Russian dudes who were currently indulged in a game of cards.

"Let me handle this, dudes," Eddie said enthusiastically. "I've been itching for some action."

"All yours," cheered Ray.

Eddie snuck up towards the two of them and landed a sick spinning kick on one's head and immediately put a bind on the other, to prevent him from raising an alarm.

But, they were tough Russian dudes. They put up a good fight, but none for Eddie. Perfectly dodging both their punches and kicks simultaneously, he made mincemeat out of them.

"You're too energetic man," joked Ray.

Eddie chuckled.

They exited into the world, upbeat about their success, but what followed made all those emotions vanish. They found themselves surrounded by around twenty men, all with clubs and bats, some even with revolvers hungry for their blood.

"But…how?" Eddie was shocked.

"Are you afraid you cannot take them down muscle head?" taunted Ray.

"NEVER!" Eddie shouted as he charged towards the left side of the crowd.

Ray followed behind as he dashed towards the right.

Clearly, they were wolves preying on the sheep. While Ray showed a calm and collected way of fighting which was truly elegant to watch, Eddie was much more loosely wired and brutal. They went through all of them as quickly as Eminem through his verses.

Just then, Ray was shot. Given his instinctive abilities, he jumped, but due to the bullet being targeted at his lower belly, it struck him in his thigh and was deep enough to immobilize him. That was definitely the work of a master marksman

"RAY," shouted Eddie as he turned towards the apprehender. "BLAZER! WHY? I AM GOING TO KILL YOU!"

"HAHAHA! As if you weakling could do anything to me. As if any of you fools could do anything to me. You insolent little brats. I had you grabbed by the back of your neck and you brats just kept going forward with it. HAHAHA!" Blazer laughed maniacally.

Just as Eddie was about to charge toward Blazer, Cain contacted him, "Team Arrow. About 10 jeeps and trucks are headed your way. Run. Stat."

"Cain… Ray's been shot. Blazer has turned on us. I will need backup."

"Wait there's no time for that. Just run from there. I'll take care of Ray… Don't worry, I cut Blazer from our call just now. He didn't hear any of this." Cain acted quickly.

Hearing this, without a second thought, Eddie ran, placing his complete trust in his friends.

"No, you don't," shouted Blazer as he chased him, completely forgetting about Ray.

Just as they left, Ollie and George arrived to collect Ray who was on the brink of unconsciousness. They collected Cain and rushed with full speed out of the city.

"Dude, this had poison in it. Look, his whole thigh has gone purple," Ollie said as he examined the spot where the bullet had hit Ray.

"I'll be f…fine. Just focus on getting Eddie," Ray said with heavy breaths while wrapping a scrap of his now-cut T-shirt tightly around his wound.

Meanwhile, Eddie was running for his life, with Blazer chasing him with his fangs out. Both of them ran all over the town, jumping from house to house, roof to roof, breaking into shops and the whole shebang.

Eventually, they landed on the highway and started running in a straight line; a cat-and-mouse chase! This gave Blazer a chance to catch up. He was clearly superior to Eddie in terms of both experience and ability.

He latched onto Eddie from behind and got in a nice right hook. But Eddie was able to recover and slip from Blazer's clutch.

"Look's like I have no choice but take you down, you traitor." Eddie was clearly furious.

What followed was a showdown between two men out for blood. An epic display of hand-to-hand combat. Blazer's bulky ferocity against the smoothness and rage of Eddie's power.

But as the fight proceeded, it turned ugly for Eddie. Blazer was overpowering him with sheer brute force. He was toying with Eddie as though he was the Hulk playing with Loki. The only thing keeping him alive as Blazer tore through him was Eddie's unfathomable anger and will for revenge.

Making their way towards here were the other four who were now being chased by a fleet of cars all raining hell on them.

George, a master on the wheel, rushed through the town trying to bait and lose the ones in pursuit. He had all the roadways, shortcuts, and alleyways of the town carved in his memory beforehand. Nobody would deem him to be a first-timer in the town.

"Alright everyone, hang on to your lives," said George, as he stepped on the accelerator.

He suddenly took a sharp turn and entered an alley that wasn't exactly made for a car to travel. Blasting through the lined-up carts and numerous boxes, he broke out from the other side to arrive at the location where the brawl between Eddie and Blazer was going down. He ran over Blazer, who was standingbeside an unconscious Eddie.

Blazer was blasted backward from the impact with a force that would definitely kill had it been anybody else. Although injured, he wasn't dead. Nevertheless, he started to get back on his feet to tear the car apart, but he had been got good in the leg and struggled to stand up.

This was the cure for their escape. Without any chance of fighting and winning, they had no choice but to run. They collected Eddie and blasted off. They were down two men and the other three alone were in no shape to rake on a potential force of hundreds, which was starting to catch up behind them.

George blasted the pedal and they went off atfull speed…

It has been three hours since. It was almost night. "Finally lost them." George took a deep breath of relief.

Everyone was too exhausted to say anything. So they just passed down a little nod as George continued to drive into oblivion.

CHAPTER 3

Once again, I was lying there unable to move, just like in past days. How many had it been, since I first woke up? I haven't got the slightest clue. Also, why aren't I getting any better? It's like my health keeps on regressing. Every time I wake up again, my head feels as heavy as a large truck if you filled it with elephants; and my body felt completely numb.

"Oh, you're awake, bro."

I had forgotten about that man for a moment.

I tried to speak but my efforts were in vain. "Take it easy, man. You should not be moving at all with your condition."

That's exactly what I wanted to know. What happened to me and who was this man and where I was now? So many questions flooded my head and it felt like it would explode any moment now.

That's when he fed me some water. My whole core calmed down. I tried looking outside. It was night time and I could see into the vast scenery from where we were. We must have been on a really high floor.

"Alright, do you wanna continue with the story then?"he asked me. That's when I recalled the story, he had been telling me. About the 5 NOVA and Russian facilities. It felt like something straight out of a sci-fi novel but it's not like I had anything better, or as a matter of fact, anything else to do.

After an approximate drive of sevenhours, and around 600 kilometers of traveling, the five reached Cherepovets which was home to an international airport but wasn't too well known.

"But George, it's been seven hours. Surely, they would have anticipated us getting here. It's not very popularplus it's the closest." Ollie raised a valid point.

"Only it's net, you see, there are numerous airports in the vicinity of St. Petersburg. But obviously, both we and NOVA know it's impossible for us to use them. Now, the closest airport to St. Petersburg is around 300 km away from it. So, I deliberately chose Cheropovets," George explained with a satisfied look on his face.

Eddie had been badly injured. During their drive, he had been stuck in the realm between consciousness and unconsciousness. He finally came to his senses when the boys proceeded to carry him out of the car.

Now that they were there, this left the problem of them getting out of there. In a county like Russia, with such strict rules, this would be impossible.

Fortunately for them, Cain came to the rescue. His brother Adam, who had been serving in the US Air Force and had prominent influence there, was able to bring a helicopterout there. He was set to meet Cain and the others in the nearest town.

"Yo, what up dawg," Cain's brother had a deep scorching voice, but it was lively.

"Yo, brother." Cain wasthe polar opposite of his brother, in terms of him always being calm and collected, deep in thought.

"I can't thank you enough for coming out there, sir," Ray expressed his gratitude. "It must have been quite difficult, this process."

"You bet, dude. Anyway, it's all good. Anything for the group of prodigies. But you lot, what happened." Your message was too vague. What are ya'll doing there in Russia,", Adam's expression turned completely serious, showing his experience in the army.

"It's quite a lot, and I'm not fond of discussing it here and right now. Let's hurry and get out of here. We can talk once we get to the States," Ray explained.

"Yeah… Yeah…You're right man. Let's go."

The plan was to introduce them as trusted friends at the airport. As the security guys were already on strict orders to not mess up anything with the "American army man", they might let them through.

It was a gamble but it had a good chance of weighing out.

And it did. Due to all of them having passports and all documents stating valid reasons for travel, they were not put under suspicion and were allowed to fly back with Adam.

They were able to take off just fine, escaping the evil of NOVA and Blazer.

After landing in the US, they were summoned by an army Sargent to explain their actions in Russia. After all, they were soldiers and they knew that violence in a foreign country could have been well led to implications for the whole country.

The fivethen went to Los Angeles, where the Sergeant was currently residing in.

"The city of dreams. The old guy seems to have colorful ambitions," George said jokingly.

"You bet," said Adam. "I'd say they are mostly green. Hahaha." Both of them exchanged chuckles.

After a drive, they all reached a humongous mansion, home to a gazillion fountains.

Upon entering, the five of them were accompanied to the first floor and subsequently to a large empty room. Unfortunately, Adam was not allowed to go with them and they parted ways outside the building.

The guy from the security who had led them to the room tells them, "Please wait in here. I'll just inform Sir Bradly."

He went off and came back after five minutes to escort them.

After a long walk through the ravishing monument, they entered a hall where a man who must've been in his early 50s and a completely bald dude, was playing snooker.

"Don't say a word and go sit down," the guy, presumably Bradly, said without even looking at them.

He then continued to finish his game and that too with admirable skill. After their game, the bald guy left after his goodbyes and with an uncanny glance toward the five.

When it was just the sixof us left, Ollie suddenly said, "You're quite good at it…huh…wanna bash heads for once?"

"Keep quiet, you insolvent brat. Know your place and especially after what you've all done. Just who do you think you are, invading Russia and on top of that starting a brawl there? I don't give a damn about your talent or anything else. Just know this, if I get even a glance of you all being in the gray, the morning sun would be rising at least fiveless people," the Sarge was agitated. He had a wrinkly face and a scratchy voice, almost like his voice made pit stops in between.

After a deafening silence of thirty seconds, Ray responded.

"Sir, I completely understand the position we're in. But we refuse to be ashamed of our actions."

Bradly raised his eyebrows and looked at Ray from the corner of his eyes, in disbelief at the insolence of the kid.

As Bradly was about rain hell on Ray, he continued. "It's because we have confirmed the existence of a terrorist society, which also happens to be behind the Italy bombings."

Bradly said nothing as if waiting to hear more.

Ray started to elaborate, "When the blasts happened in Italy, luckily, we happened to be nearby. So, naturally, we went to investigate. On-site, we crossed roads with Blazer."

Bradly was astounded. That was a name he didn't expect to hear. But the dumbfoundedness on his face disappeared just as quickly as it had sprouted.

"And as it turned out, Blazer happened to have some info about the whole mess. So, we started working together. And that was our only mistake."

The old Sargent looked like he was expecting to hear something like this. He then mockingly said, "And Blazer, and keep in mind, a dead person, gave you info on this so-called "terrorist society," he laughed.

Cain spurted in anger, "Take it seriously. You do not believe in this, do you? Well, guess what, Ray and Eddie managed to get into one of their factories in Russia. And it was incomprehensibly huge. So much so that, if this group decided to go for any country, it can destroy it from its very roots."

Bradly continued to laugh and suddenly shifted to a more serious tone, "Shut your traps, you fool. Do you not know anything, lads? Italy has already declared the blasts to be due to defective pieces which were being transported by their army. Honestly, how naïve can one get."

None of the fivecould speak. What was going on? They were shocked out of their minds.

"Now get out of my sight, you all. And just try and do something funny again and I will see to it that your fat skulls are at the bottom of an ocean."

Ray, George, Ollie, and Cain's faces were those of shock and anger. But they couldn't have done anything there.

They were led outside the mansion and were put on their way to the airport by an army car.

Back in New Jersey, where they were currently posted, they decided to hold a proper meeting to go over things.

As they entered the room, Eddie, who had not uttered a single word since flying back from Russia, punched the wall to leave huge cracks. He then exploded out of his mind, smashing things helter-skelter. All of that frustration he had from the NOVA, Bradly, and on top of everything else, Blazer.

"I am going to finish that bastard," he shouted as he split a table in half.

"Knew this was coming," said Ray.

"Alright, let's calm down, Eddie. Shall we?" Cain tried to step in.

After he defeated the final boss aka the vase, Eddie stopped and left the room; his face-no less red than a tomato.

As Cain was about to leave to get him back, Ray stopped him, "He's not going to budge whatsoever right now. Let's continue among ourselves and we'll fill in him later."

They all sat down among the war spoils of Eddie vs the room and Ollie started to summarize the past months of their lives. "So, alright guys. Let's first of all cheer up. This is no time to be gloomy and stuff bro."

All four of them chuckled and the room lit up.

"Hmmmmm… let's see…"

Ring…Ring…

It was George's. He picked up and after two minutes of complete silence said, "Are you sure? .... alright," and hung up.

"So, who was it George?" Ollie asked.

George did not say anything, then smiled and said, "Guys, it was someone from the army. He said…"

"Don't say any names. I'm from the army and saw you all at the Sarge's house. Now, listen carefully, there is some activity from the NOVA group in Arizona, and one of my trusted sources has told me, they have an open window on the 27th at the Grand Canyon."

"Guys, this is exactly what we need right now."

Ollie asked, "How can we trust this guy, though? What if, what happened before…"

It's because he knew about us being at Bradly's house. First of all, no one outside would know it to be an army base, and secondly, no one except the people present there would know of our visit," Ray explained calmly.

"Yeah…right."

Ray continued, "Anyway, this is quite an interesting turn out of events. But still looking back in Russia, it might be impossible for us to handle. And by the looks of its army help will be scarce. We will have to come up with quite a plan."

Ollie said, "Alright, today is the 19th. We have roughly a week left. Let's put our heads to work."

Four of them started working on a plan to knock the socks out of NOVA. During this time, Eddie spent most of his day training his body, dreading defeat at the hands of Blazer. Deep down, he couldn't comprehend the reason forBlazer's betrayal. A man who was so dedicated to the country, so much as to lay his life on the battlefield, now working as a terrorist.

He was approached by the others several times, who came to stop him from overexerting himself. I mean, exercising fifteen hours a day can never be healthy.

But he cut them all off for fourdays after which he stopped his madness. Having pushed his body to the limit, he probably lost more than he gained.

His body was all red and he could barely breathe as he lay there on the ground. The thunderstorm inhis mind had gotten quieter but it was still very well there, looking to steer him for his next actions.

"Not changed at all, are we?" Ray came to see him for the first time in four days.

"Hm…shut up…a…and get me some…water…water."

"Dude, look at yourself. What you need right now is a day in your bed with a drip up your…'" Ray said as he went to pick Eddie up.

As he picked him up, after an attempt to struggle, Eddie gave in and fainted.

When he woke up, he was in his bed, dripped up with glucose and surrounded by his four friends who were chatting and laughing.

On seeing him, they turned serious.

"I'll probably never see a bigger idiot in my life," Ollie joked.

"Unless this guy evolves,"said George.

Everybody including Eddie burst into laughter.

"I'm sorry, guys," Eddie seemed to have calmed down a bit more.

"It's alright man. Recover quickly. We'll be needing your ability for this upcoming storm," said Cain in a serious tone.

"Fill me in. What's up?"

George started explaining, "Basically, in about 5 days from now, someone from NOVA is gonna surface in Arizona, and the plan is just to kick their bottoms."

"Sounds like a good plan," Eddie was excited.

"I wish," George continued. "The only problem is manpower. You know what happened four days ago. There's no way we're gonna get a unit to be able to stand up against them, and after seeing them in Russia, we're definitely gonna need one."

"We've been trying to secure a unit for the past fourdays, but everyone is dodging us," said Ollie.

"Hmm… Let me try something here boys. Don't get your hopes too high, but I might be able to manage around ten men. I have an old friend in the army who owes me one. He was two years senior to me and Ray back in army school. The thing is, he is in charge of a squad of only ten. But he'll be able to deliver," Eddie was confident.

"That dude, huh," said Ray.

After a long twenty minutes of Eddie explaining the whole thing to a 'Brett', he finally hung up the phone and said, "Well lads, here's the thing. I have news from both sides of the coin. So, he agreed to come out there but his squadron is currently reduced to seven including himself due to a recent shootout."

"Well, we'll have to make do with whatever we can get," said Cain. "Let's get equipped for the fight ourselves, and Eddie get a good day and night's rest."

Skip past five days and it was the day of reckoning. Right now, the only way to cross the Grand Canyon was its oldest constructed bridge, dating back thirty years. All the rest of the passageways were closed off for upgrading purposes.

This road was not fully metaled and the majority of the surrounding place was loose dirt.

At the end where the confrontation was to take place, were a few buildings, which were emptied that day by the US army unit of twelve members.

All of them hid in a separate building in units of three and waited for the bread to arrive.

At about noon, in the scorching sun, there arrived a grand fleet of about twenty cars and a helicopter. This was, without a doubt, the NOVA group.

As the front car was a few meters fromgetting off the bridge, the explosives that were set there went off and fourcars in the front went flying off into the 4,000-foot canyon.

It caused panic among them as they flung out of formation and some stopped abruptly. After half a minute, a lot of the people started coming out, fully armed; probably after getting orders, from their superior.

This is when the second phase of the five's plan was set in motion. Having anticipated a large force, George rushed in with a Jeep and started drifting in full circles to cause a sort of a sand devil there, causing loss of vision for the NOVA army.

That's when the rest of the crew went in fully "tech-ed" up and caused a slaughter.

While George kept drifting, the NOVA army was swallowed in the cloud by the rest of them.

Just then, amidst all the panic and shooting, a rocket flew from the helicopter, roughly where George's car was; and it sent him flying towards the edge.

The fighting suddenly stopped as everybody tried to consume information aboutwhat just happened.

George's car flipped thrice and landed upside down. A fully battered and bleeding George slid out of the car and laid there on the floor unconscious. Everyone was shocked, but they did not have time on their hands.

The fight resumed, now with Brett's unit starting to retreat to the buildings for cover.

During the whole process, threeof them were shot but the other foursuccessfully reached back.

Out of breath, Brett tried to contact headquarters, "This is Agent Fox. Request for backup at Grand Canyon Passage 01. Terrorist Attack. Over."

"…Yeah…Agent Fox… This is headquarters. Sending a unit ASAP. Minimum ETA 12 minutes. Over."

This was too long, and they knew it. They started shooting from the buildings, slowly chopping off the army from a distance.

Meanwhile, Eddie, Ray, George, and Ollie battled at the frontlines, up close, displaying their superior abilities. Loose sand, dozens of cars, and panic aided them as well.

As the opposition's numbers were reduced, Ollie was blasted off by a punch from amidst the still presiding flying sand.

As the sand settled down, standing there, laughing menacingly was none other than Blazer.

"You damn BASTARD. What are you doing here?" Eddie charged toward the traitor without a second thought.

"You impudent fools. Thinking you can get one up on us. Pipe down, boys, and enjoy as I SLAUGHTER YOU ALL," said Blazer as he stopped Eddie's punch midway and kicked him in the gut to push him off his balance.

He then, as he stated, started to slaughter the rest of them.

Ollie charged toward him and tried to slide past his lead to attack from behind but Blazer, despite his heavy structure, caught his punch midway, twisted his arm, and shoved him in the chest to knock Ollie back.

Next on the card were Ray and Eddie, who were previously busy fighting the rest of their foot-soldiers.

"Bring it ONN!" shouted Blazer as he continued his maniacal laugh.

Both Ray and Eddie charged together towards the human truck only to be blocked by him and pushed back. Nevertheless, they continued their assault, showing unbelievable coordination throughout their attacks. It was as if they were being operated through the same strings.

Their continuous attack finally broke Blazer's hold over the fight and drives him into a corner. Now, he was on the short end of the stick.

As perfectly dodged his hooks, he gutted Blazer into the stomach to throw him off his balance. Just then Eddie leapt toward his legs and made him fall tohis knees.

As Ray was about to deliver a full round of kicks to his face, multiple shots hit his leg and abdomen, more rounds were shot, this time towards Eddie who dodged them until he took cover behind a car.

The bullets did not stop raining onEddie. He sat there with no opening whatsoever, shouting and calling for Ray who lay fifteen meters from him, barely conscious.

The shooting suddenly stopped. Eddie peeked from behind the car, which was now following apart, thanks to the shower before. He saw Blazer had recovered and now standing up. Beside him, was a slender-looking man in full black clothes. His clean shaved face was a huge contrast to his suit.

With the most wicked smile, Eddie had ever seen, he started to move forward, stopped after a few steps, and said, with a deep voice, completely contrasting his sleek look, "Welcome to my world, Americans. Zuck, get one behind the car," now in a more sinister voice, "Do not kill him yet, just toy with him. Break him. I'll give him the final blow worse than death. Make sure he can't move."

"Yes, Mr. O."

Eddie was too shocked to gather in all that this 'Mr. O' said. But he wondered why was Blazer called Zuck, and who was this MGK-looking freak.

As his brain was processing this info, Blazer smashed the car from the top, and some of the debris blasted Eddie in the face.

Blazer went for Eddie next. He tried to counter but Blazer was in rage mode, screaming all over, his eyes all white, pupils barely visible.

Blocking Eddie's every attack and returning double the amount, at this point he was just manhandling him.

After a heavy kick to knock him down, Blazer (or Zuck, apparently) started repeatedly punching his face. Eddie was no better than a punctured punching bag for Zuck. Satisfying his desire of the fist, Zuck picked up Eddie's leg and slowly twisted it backward, and in the end, snapped it quickly to dislocate it.

Eddie let out screeches as he writhed in pain.

Zuck picked him up through the skull and while shouting smashed Eddie into the ground for the final blow.

This was it. Eddie was no longer in any condition to speak, let alone move. All he could manage was to keep his eyes slightly open, that too with a fuzzy vision.

What he could make out at that moment was a black figure, probably Mr. O moving towards where Ray was lying.

Eddie felt his eardrums ringing, not able to hear anything else when suddenly Zuck picked him up and he slightly regained his senses.

He could now make out Mr. O's evil laughter as he dragged on unconscious Ray towards the edge.

He was planning to throw him down. Oh no! Eddie had to stop him. Nobody else was there. For some reason, even Brett's unit wasn't there.

Eddie tried to scream, but nothing came out of him. He hung there helplessly as his best mate was heading towards the depth of the Grand Canyon.

Standing at the edge, Mr. O, laughing atthe top of his lungs, held Ray over the valley and gave him a straight kick to throw him down.

"How'd you like that, long hair?" he laughed taunting Eddie.

Eddie tried to scream with his whole might, but out came just a low screech, as both Zuck and Mr. O were laughing.

Suddenly, Nr. O stopped, raised his eyebrows widened his eyes, and with a sinister hushed voice said, "I've got an idea. Hee…hee…hee…hee." Now in a louder, more normal voice, he said, "You know Zuck, food gets stuck in my teeth and I try to use a…toothpick, my teeth always end up breaking it."

"Been there, done that…sir," said Zuck, still deep in laughter.

Mr. O continued, "Zucky boy, don't you think these fivehere are just like toothpicks? But not just any toothpicks. No…no…no… They are toothpicks I like to break. First, chew them and then" *imitates breaking* "bye-bye."

As he was saying this, Mr. O made his way to the wreck. It was George's. Without a single thought again, he picked up George and dropped it in the valley near where Ray was dropped. "Toothpick no.2, he said making chewing gestures. Eddie was screaming and fighting from the inside. But the truth is, he was reduced to a mere spectator right now.

After dropping George off the edge, Mr. O now started moving toward one of the last twocars of the fleet. What was he planning now?

Eddie had stopped struggling. He had expended all little energy he had. Right now, in light of his two friends being at the bottom of the Grand Canyon, he was unable to think straight. He just hung there — his life in Zuck's hands, literally.

Mr. O's car started moving. Oh my God! It was headed towards Ollie and Cain, who still lay unconscious from Zuck's attack. You could sense the evil laugh of the man even through closed, blacked-out windows.

But as it was closing on Ollie, a loud voice of sirens filled the gloomy place.

There it is, the army. They finally arrived. But was it too late?

Mr. O's car, nevertheless, kept going and ran over Ollie at full speed, crushing multiple bones, and probably killing him.

But the NOVA could not neglect the gathering armed forces. So, Mr. O stepped out and the helicopter, in which he came here in the firstplace; lowered itself to let the guy abroad.

Zuck at the same time threw Eddie and ran towards the chopper as gunshots started raining. He made it and they escaped successfully since the army didn't bring any aired vehicles.

Three of the fivelay there, on the brink of life and death, and two others were pushed towards the dark end. And on top of that, Eddie saw it first-hand while being unable to do anything. He was fully broken from the inside as well as outside.

Yeah, the army arrived. But the damage was already done. For the three that were recovered by the medic team, everything was over by a mile.

CHAPTER 4

Just woke up. I'm starting to get the hang of it. Of breathing, of seeing. My head hurts but anyway, things are better.

I tried looking around, and saw the man from the corner of my eye, working on something, but I couldn't see what it was.

Seeing me awake, he stopped what he was doing and came over to me.

"You're awake already, huh? You usually pass out for a couple of days. Progress, dude. Progress. Anyway, how are ya feeling?"

I tried to speak, but I must've not recovered as much as I thought, because all that came out was, "I…m…be…er."

"Let's not push ourselves, shall we? Here drink this, you'll feel better."

He handed me a glass of water. As the water went down my throat, I felt much better.

"So, let's continue now," he said, and pulled up a chair and sat next to where I lay.

Absolute devastation had set into the lives of Eddie, Cain, and Ollie as they lay in hospital beds in face of their crushing defeat and top of everything the loss of Ray and George.

But they werecapable of doing nothing at that point in time. Anger and frustration were ruling their minds.

5 months later-----

After their brutal defeat, the remaining three members of the squad were left in pretty bad shape.

As of this day, Eddie and Cain have recovered from their injuries.

Eddie though had not recovered emotionally. Still very much in reminiscence of both his friends, especially Ray, whom he had lived with for almost his entire life, he was not taking it easy, or even normal, you could say. He spent most of his time training his body, in order to defeat his former captain Blazer, who was called Zuck. Working out day and night he hoped to raise his physical abilities and battle to not feel helpless and unable to save those near him, unlike the Eddie from five months ago did.

Cain accepted the defeat more graciously than Eddie. Still wanting to improve, he began training to sharpen his marksman abilities. Close range, snipers, rifles, automatic guns, and the whole shebang.

A major heartbreaker was a drastic revelation for Ollie. In light of him being trampled over by a whole car, he had suffered some permanent damage to his legs.

Legs, the most important thing, arguably, for an agent like so, stripped away. Nevertheless, he found solace in working from the desk. Having transformed into a full techie in the past few years, he tremendously developed the information-gathering sector of their team. Tracking, tracing, hacking, you name it.

So, this brings us to the reason for this five-month skip. What has happened now?

In these past fivemonths, there have been numerous bomb blasts all over the world. All of which were unresolved cases. But they had one thing in common. Ollie was able to trace several of these bomb blasts to Japan, from either the transporting route or some Japan-exclusive material found on sites. Last week, to fuel his suspicions, he received a lead from the same army dude who had informed them about the Grand Canyon incident. He called and said, "Hey bro, what's up. It's me, the guy you met in a restaurant in Arizona during your Canyon visit. It's been a long time. You should try ramen sometime," and then hung up.

Arizona-Canyon, Ollie understood who the guy was. But the cream of the info lay in the word 'ramen'.

That's it. Ramen. Japanese. Japan. Ollie was able to further his lead to establish a connection to Japan. That meant, there was probably a major facility of NOVA there, seeing the number of linking cases.

Just as Ollie was working on this lead, the army got a notification about a bomb discovered here in New Jersey.

This was their time to shine. The three responded to the callout and confirmed their status as approaching the site.

Eddie and Cain rushed out of the building. Waiting for them, was an absolute beauty, a custom 2022 Dodge challenge which was a 20-year-old model, but due to a customs job, a beast no less. They stopped making muscle cars like this.

With the sweet vrooms of the engine, they went off to the site where the bomb was located.

Steaming through the traffic with their superior car, they reached the place in no time.

Unfortunately for them, they had only about two minutes before it went off.

"Two minutes is too long, bro. Give me a better challenge here," said Eddie while approaching the bomb, all suited up.

"Well, you've got your wish on your plate, Eddie," said Ollie through the comms. "This system is quite complex. Give me a minute till I figure this out."

Cain carefully opened the bomb to expose its digital circuit.

Meanwhile, Ollie ran an algorithm to find out how to break the circuit.

Now the situation was turning tense. They might run out of time. Suddenly, Ollie hit upon the combination, "Yeah, got it, Eddie. Sending it to your watchpad. Dude, you have to be faster than your whip on this one. It has fifty-seven steps and you have less than thirty seconds now.

"Leave it to me,"said Eddie as he memorized the pattern.

Twenty-six seconds to go.

He started to fill it in. Once he joined the first two dots there was no going back. He couldn't mess it up or potentially the whole block could blow up.

What followed was an unbelievable feat. He, without another thought, sped through the combinations as if he was practicing for it his whole life. The wiring of the bomb was revealed.

Ollie announced again, "Yellow, red, blue, green, black."

Four seconds left.

Cain quickly cut the wires in the order and with just one second left, the bomb was diffused.

All the army men gathered (there was only a handful), applauded, and cheered as both Eddie and Cain boarded their car and set off.

Back in their headquarters, aka their dorm room, the three sat down to discuss their plan going forward.

"This was without a doubt, a bomb from NOVA. I analyzed the bomb you brought back and its material composition almost matches the scrap pieces found in Munich, Germany, a month ago, Punjab, India, two months ago, and Cape Town, South Africa four months ago," explained Ollie.

"Alright then. What's the status with the lead you got," enquired Cain.

"Well, that's the interesting part. Activity is basically confirmed in Japan," replied Ollie.

"Basically?"

"Yeah. So, the thing is, a lot of the debris found from the bombing sites of the past months somehow leads back to Japanese origin in different ways. Also, remember the guy who informed us about the Canyon incident."

Eddie raised his eyebrows hearing the "Canyon incident".

"He contacted me through a code, basically confirming Japan to be linked to NOVA."

"So, what's the plan now?" Eddie said in a very serious tone. You could tell the scene of the Grand Canyon was playing right now in his mind.

"Well, the plan's very very simple. I have arranged for us a meeting with a guy in NOVA," Ollie said nonchalantly.

"What?" said both in unison.

"Take it easy guys. Through different identities, I've registered us three for a meeting with a NOVA employer in Japan in four days," Ollie looked proud of himself.

"So, you booked an employer in Japan. But you said you were not 100% confirmed about Japan. So, how does that work?" asked Cain.

"Mate, it's NOVA we're talking about. It's arguably the biggest organization in the world right now. Do you think, a meeting in Japan means anything to do with the place of employment…" After a pause, a deep breath, and the vanishing of his proud look, Ollie continued.

"This brings me to the biggest gamble of this plan. So, as I said before, going there we do not know where we will get hired, and it might not be Japan.

"Even then it's alright innit. Wherever we get posted, we'll have a place to investigate plus that leaves Japan as a whole another chapter," said Eddie.

"It's not that simple, mate. You see, my gut tells me Japan is gonna be the key to this chest. And this access that we have gotten as NOVA employees is at most temporary. It was possible to get, due to the incident five months ago in the first place. That geezer Bradly ignored a potential threat to the country which paid in the form of the success of whatever NOVA had to do that day, wipe out of Brett's unit, and subsequent blasts in five different American dead. So, they agreed to assist this mission…"

"But this damn NOVA is a damn hard nut to crack. So… it won't be long before they discover our piracy," Eddie cut in.

"On point."

Cain then asked, "How long are we talking?"

"A month…a month and a half if we're lucky. Although, that's highly unlikely."

Eddie spoke after exiting his deep thoughts, "Let's request a unit to be gathered for a full attack on the facility. We can enter a facility in Japan if it's there. They'll start flying over a few days after we leave; that too in small chunks spread over two or three weeks. If we end up with naught, we dissolve the mission."

"That's actually really good. But managing a very large unit would be really difficult on this short a notice," said Cain.

"Well, we'll just have to try our best," cheered Ollie.

Just like that, the boys were set for Japan.

On the night before their flight — "So boys, here you go," said Ollie as he handed over new passports, IDs, and transparent masks to Eddie and Cain.

As they put on their masks, the whole of their faces completely transformed. Even their hair looked completely different. Ollie went on to give a complete bodysuit of the same type to both of them. There was no cutting corners.

"This suit is equipped with a full voice modifier and BO modifier in case our smells are examined."

"Dude, this is genius," Cain looked excited, which was very unlike his usual calm demeanor.

The day of the flight. All negotiations with the army were on board. The assistance unit requested was agreed to and was in process of assembly. Now, the rest of the plan was largely up to luck. Luck, as in getting into the Japanese facility. The three of them felt like high school students, looking to get into their dream college, just up the stakes by 10 thousand.

After a long flight, it was time for the city of *Otakus*, one of the largest metropolitan cities, Tokyo. A bonus was that their flight landed at night, so the views from the plane were mesmerizing.

But the three were not there for sightseeing. Their mission was crystal clear in their heads. They were supposed to meet the employer at 3:30 in the morning. They checked into their hotel and waited for the big hour.

They deliberately did not go to bed that night, just to appear a little sleepy before the interview.

The "science" behind this was as Eddie explained a few days back during their meeting.

"So, the probable reason for the meeting to be at such an odd time is in accordance with the first level of secret examination only some army units of the United States practice for non-combatants. It is basically a very simple check. They check your activeness or more precisely your sleepiness."

Even Ollie and George were amused at hearing this. "Basically, it might show previous expertise or ability to be perfectly active at an odd hour. Also, as it is based on speculation, no one is dropped, except the too sleepy ones of course. But the too active people are looked into more carefully for a potential infiltration. It is a level 1 test and not practised much solely because experienced intruders are generally aware of it and do what we are going to do. Not sleep for the entire previous day and subsequent night. Given our physique and training, we will probably not get too sleepy but drained enough to appear normal people looking to work."

And that is exactly how it turned out.

At 3:30 in the morning, they were called to a warehouse on the edge of the city. It was a large one on the surface, this time unlike the one in Russia.

Blazing through the empty streets of Tokyo, they finally reached the warehouse.

On reaching the door, a guy opened it as they were about to knock with heavy eyes, and a dad-bod, he asked, "*Nani?*" (Which is Japanese for "What?")

Eddie answered, in Japanese as well, "The price of the grains is going to drop today". This was the code for identifying themselves, which Ollie had received just an hour ago.

He led them in. The place looked even bigger from the inside, probably becauseit was quite empty, for a large warehouse. Even then, there were a lot of crates lined up and bags full of seeds and other grains which took them back to the Russian storehouse.

Apart from the lousy lighting in the main hall, there was just one room on the right side and bright white light shone through the half-open door.

The three were made to enter the room after which the guy locked them in.

As if the light wasn't enough before, another blinding white light was switched on. The room gave the vibes of solitary confinement with nothing but whiteness all around.

"Welcome," a deep voice, probably modified, reverbed throughout the room, "So you're the ones applying for the weapon design unit, huh...?"

And just like this, the announcer asked them some questions about their past experiences and stuff like that.

And as expected, all three perfectly answered all questions, getting stuck up at one or two places, deliberately of course.

After the questioning, he said, out of the blue, "Alright then, start working from today itself. Breakfast and dinner will be only for half an hour each. Dinner at 8:30 and breakfast at 7:00. Start working at 5:00 in the morning, and your shift ends at midnight. No excuses. No holiday."

Those working conditions were interesting. I'll stop at that.

Nevertheless, the guard came back to take the three shocked Americans outside. Again, they acted like they were a bit shocked athearing those conditions even though they knew it was the best NOVA would possibly offer.

They were then taken into another room, where they were thoroughly checked. And by 'thoroughly', I mean, they had to take off their clothes, their hair got pulled, and whatnot. Carrying and bag or any personal items were forbidden.

After dressing up again, another dude came in this time more well-built than the previous one. He told them (in English), "You'll be working here in Tokyo itself. Follow me."

This caught the three-off guard. This was totally out of the blue. But… They were bursting from the inside. They did it. They somehow got what they wanted. This was very well the best-case scenario.

The new dude, while leading them somewhere informed them of their duties and then said, "The unit you'll be assigned already has two people working there. They've been here for around a month so ask them what you want to do. Don't disturb me. Never understood."

"Yes, sir," in unison.

He led them to a corner of the warehouse, climbed the small pile of crates there, and reached the three-box-high corner pile. He alone moved all the loaded boxes aside and revealed the floor beneath. It looked like an ordinary floor.

He then made the three of them wear blindfolds and turned them towards the other side. He then went on to do something. All the three heard were rapid footsteps. It was probably some kind of code, because they took their blindfold off, on the dude's prompt, the floor revealed itself to be an entrance to a pod-like thing.

They jumped in first followed by the dude. The pod started its descent.

As they sat face to face, Eddie closely observed the guy who brought them there. His name was 'Katakuri'. He had a chiseled body which was evident through his tight swampy green t-shirt. To go with the t-shirt, he was wearing a brown cut-sleeve jacket and black pants. He had a skinny face and dark big eyes, and dark spiky hair to go with them.

Just then, the pod stopped. They were here. And the sight before them left them bamboozled and frozen in their steps.

The pod reached there so fast, that they didn't notice it at all, but the factory infront of them was about 200 feet tall and stretched into an infinite void. Thousands upon thousands of people working like pigs. Running about, without proper nutrition and next to no pay.

Katakuri said, "Stop daydreaming and follow me."

He led them through the facility. Ollie noticed the side walls further branding into narrow alleys, each with a unique number and many with the same color.

After walking a fair bit, Katakuri took a left to enter lane 68 which had a passage with blue lighting.

"Here, as you saw the lanes are color coded. Muddy white for the peasantry, workers at the lowest rung of the ladder. Then the blue color, which isone rank higher.

They are mostly skilled jobs like you three, designing, etc. then there are people like me, supervisors, and other management. We have the colour black. Above us is purple…"

"But, there were no purple lanes out…" Ollie said.

Katakuri said in a louder tone, "Let me finish what I have to say first. So, above black is purple. The color of the rich. You'll not see any purple passageway. It is only for the ones at the top of this ladder. The leaders and theones they keep close to themselves. Write this with fire in your head. Do not try to enter a color higher than yours unless you have a death wish."

He led them to their place of work and the left. The door was already open.

Cain said, "If I'm right, he did mention two other people working here. "(In a quieter voice), "We have to watch out for them. They'll be the ones closest to us".

They entered the room to find the whole place covered with loose papers, empty bottles, and microwave food boxes.

It was no better than a spoiled teenager's room.

Working there were a man and a woman, about the same age as them. The guy was buried in his computer making some designs. He wore glasses, was very skinny and had overgrown messy hair, and wore tight clothes, a t-shirt, and jeans. The lady was on the floor, deep in slumber, in what was probably her night suit, a baggy sweatshirt, and shorts.

The three of them just realized it was not time for the shift to start.

They shifted the papers on the couch and sat there. The dude on the computer didn't even look back, as if completely ignoring their existence.

After a few minutes of just mouse clicking and tying sounds, Ollie chose to break the ice, "So, the colored people have to work this early, huh?"

There was no response. The three of them didn't observe any sign of him noticing them or even being aware of their existence.

Now, this could very well turn into two scenarios. Either they were up against a trained agent or he was just a total complete nerd

They thought to themselves, "If this guy is against us have to take him in with us or take him out. If he is trained like we are, he is so very good. To not give out even the slightest clue about him noticing us and fouling us. Hmmm. He got us good.

The three, exhausted, started to move towards their dorms.

The entrance was through the same room itself. Towards the right wall, two doors sat, one being used probably by these two and the other one presumably for the three.

"Talk about not being used… AT ALL."

Ollie jokingly commented on the doors and their immediate surrounding which wasso clean, you would think that nobody comes there.

They entered the room and retired straight to bed. The exhaustion from staying up the whole night finally caught up with them.

However, they were woken up by a commotion thatseemed like its origins were the dorm room. Of course, they all thought, we still have to work to do anything.

They opened the door to the now awake girl sittingon the couch and the computer dude pacing the room. As the three entered the room, the other two appeared shocked as if they hadn't known about their arrival.

Good job, guys.

Nonetheless, greetings and introductions took place.

The guy's name was Sam and the girl's Rachael.

Sam said, "Let's not waste any time and get to work". He had a weird mixed-up accent, which raised suspicions in Eddie, but he brushed it off for now. Apart from this, he was a tall, lanky fellow now wearing a white shirt and black pants for work.

The girl, Rachael didn't speak much. Even she had changed into more professional clothes, now wearing a knee-length black short skirt, also with a white shirt which definitely could have been a size bigger. Her body shape was much visible now, as her abs excelled through the tight white shirt.

The other guys changed their clothes and went off for their adventure.

The first day went away just learning about the type of work they had to do. Nothing concrete was achieved in terms of gathering info, but… that's okay. Slow and steady wins the race.

As the three of them sat in their room after a long day of work, Ollie said, "Sam and Rachael seem to be nice people… Or at least they got their first impressions on point." He chuckled. Eddie and Cain agreed.

Cain said, "We have to start gearing up now. We do not have the luxury of relaxing even for a day."

They went to bed, determined to stir up preparations for their plan the next day.

It was 4:30 in the morning. Eddie, Ollie, Cain, and Sam were in the common room already having started their work, when they heard loud noises from Rachael's room. The door then opened and as Rachael with messy hair came out, in the background a slight portion of her room was visible. And… It was worse than the mess from a blender if you fill it up to the brim and turn it on... without its lid on.

"Sorry, boys," she said and settled down at her desk.

At 5:00, as they were about to leave to work, Ollie casually threw a question at Sam, out of curiosity, "Soooo... Sam. where'd you sleep? Don't tell me...," he raised his eyebrows and chuckled.

"No... no...no. I just sleep on the couch now,", Sam was startled by the question.

"Hey man. What? Naa, you can sleep with the boys. We'll spare plenty of room for you," Ollie instantly regretted what he said. After all, if Sam moved in with them, they could not pool info for themission. This could go south.

"Nah bro. It's alright. I sleep better on the couch anyway."

Ollie was saved. He decided not to push Sam any further as normal etiquettes would want him to. He just moved on.

Now, their initial plan was to, first of all, build a sort of a "blueprint" for the facility; to try and find its structure, all the entries, exits, paths, and pathways of the pods in which they arrived along with places with less to almost no surveillance. They dedicated the next two weeks to this particular thing, at the end of which they were armed with the complete maps of around 90% of the place, at least of the observable space. There was no telling of secret spaces or hidden rooms.

Over these two weeks, their relationship with their roommates developed. They found both Sam and Rachael to be extremely smart. Both of them were quite intellectual individuals who could easily be seen as worthy drafts for the national army.

One random day, at midnight, all five gathered in the common room as they were returning from their shifts when suddenly someone blasted through the door. It was a bald dude, who must've been in his 30s. He appeared somewhat familiar to Eddie.

With a cigarette in his mouth, he slammed the large duffel bag in his hand and shouted.

"Oye, complete all this before tomorrow's shift starts."

"But, the day's already over. It is supposed to be at 12 every night. Anyway, who even are you, barging in like that? Huh, mister, you?" Rachael's pent-up frustration and exhaustion from work bubbled out like hot lava.

The bald guy looked pissed. He walked up to her and took out a pistol. It was gold-plated and long. Nobody dared to move. The three especially couldn't risk showing their ability and exposing themselves.

The bald guy grabbed Rachael's chin, forced her mouth open and placed the gun between her teeth, and said, "You damn woman. Know your place in the bottomless pile of trash. I am from the black lanes. Get that inside your rotten brain. Now, get moving and I want all of these papers handled and sorted on the stat." He then whispers to himself, "Huh, idiot. Dare say I am bald," and walks out spitting his cigarette out and puts a fresh one in his mouth.

"Are you okay, Rachael?" Sam jumped to her side.

She seemed rather unfazed, just plain angry and jaded.

"Let's just get this done with and sleep," she said as she opened the bag to reveal an overflowing river of documents.

"It'll be a long night," said Ollie as he sighed.

After about three hours, Cain finished all the work that he took up when they were dividing the work. He seemed to be done with life. He could barely keep his eyes open. Even a highly trained bomb specialist of the US army was reduced to an overworked high school teen. Anyhow, he got up and swayedall over the place and moved towards the room.

Now, a big problem with the common room here was that the two doors to the two different bedrooms were side by side, and the rooms themselves then expanded on either side. You can see where I am going with this, right?

Cain, half asleep walked towards "his room" and burst open the door.

Rachael suddenly screamed on seeing her room being flung open. Nobody had ever seen her room, except for the glimpses of its messiness whenever Rachael stepped out in the morning.

Cain too snapped out of his slumber upon seeing foreign territory, but what he saw next blew him out of his socks.

CHAPTER 5

I feel heavy-headed again. I am starting to wonder, what is happening to me? Why, when I start feeling better, I doze off and then wake up feeling like there are twenty trucks above me, crushing me and sucking everything that is left in me.

I looked around. The man was not there. Maybe he was not expecting me to wake up at that time. Then it hit me. I knew nothing about him, not even his name. Could it be that he was doing something to me? What?

My suspicion ofthe man grew. What was it that he was doing to me? Could it be something I didn't notice? I thought for awhile.

Nothing came up in my head. But this was the only plausible explanation. But why was he doing it, how do I stop him?

So many questions and too few answers.

The adrenaline rush I got from that little deduction slowly faded away as lay there waiting for the inevitable. It was then when I realized, I wasn't just laying down, I was chained, all the way from my chest, down to my feet, to the bed. My soul left my body.

Just what was this man doing to me? What had happened before I wound up here? Was my memory loss also his doing?

Just more questions.

After more minutes of anguish, the man entered the room. Shocked to see me awake, he said, "Ohh! How are you, bro? Feeling better?"

"Stop it. Just stop it. You pretensions bastard." My anger bubbled out as words, which I hadn't spoken in so long.

"Huh, what are you saying?"

"I know you are doing something. These chains as well. Who are you? What is happening?"

The expression on his face changed from shock to pure malice with a crooked smile. "Ohh! You finally noticed. How careless of me." he laughed maniacally, "Yeahhh, I'm the one who did this to you. I'm the one who brought you here." He enlarged his eyes and started talking like a maniac.

"Huhh! But…you'll have to listen to the whole story. It is true after all. And, I'll tell you a little surprise. You… and…me…We are both a part of this story. Hahahaha."

"What? You bastard. I am not going to listen to any of your bullshit anymore."

What? I am one of the people from the story. Who was I? Eddie? Ollie? Cain? Zuck? Or maybe Rachael?

As I was deep in thought, he came up to me with a glass of water in his hand.

I got it! It was the water. Only that it wasn't. He must have been drugging me.

"Come on little one. Be a good boy and drink up. Come on. Come on," the wicked grin on his face was terrifying. He had a screw loose up there.

"As if I would, you monster. Get me out of here." I tried to move my body but the chains stopped me.

His laughter-ridden face suddenly turned serious. "Are you mad? Why would I restrain you to just release you?" He began laughing again. He was the embodiment of psycho. I can't believe how normal and friendly he had been acting up until now.

"Oh man, I didn't wanna force you. I wanted to make you suffer from your hands, Hahaha! Too… bad…"

He went back to where he usually sat and came back with a syringe.

"Here we go! Time for dinner." He laughed as he shoves the injection into my arm. More than pain, the numbness spread all over my body. I wanted to scream with all the life force of my lungs but I couldn't even move my lips.

But all the pain suddenly vanished.

I was so relaxed. More relaxed than I had ever felt in my life. Was it the drug? Yeahh!

"Well then, let's continue with our story, bro."

Everyone in the room had just faced a shock. Nobody was moving even a hair on their body. It was deathly silent.

"W… why do you have blueprints of the facility and pictures of Blazer and others in your room, Rachael? Don't tell me…," Cain's voice echoed under the silence that followed.

Rachael hesitated to do anything. She had no explanation in mind. She glanced toward Sam and then smacked her belt to reveal a nanotech gun forming. She pointed it towards Cain, who already had her atgunpoint due to his faster, more advanced nanotech watch.

At this point, both Eddie and Ollie drew their respective pistols pointing them at both Rachael and Sam, who was surprisingly also a wielder.

Nobody shot. They were all shaken. Silence still reigned over the room.

Rachael chose to break the ice, "Alright let's calm down. We've got a lot happening here. Let's take it slow and talk it out."

"Go on then. Start explaining," said Eddie.

"Why should I tell you? Who are you guys, anyway and how do you have guns?" Rachael tried to gain the upper hand.

"You're in no position to talk. We outnumber you both and trust me, (with emphasis) we are quite good." Ollie took a step forward, causing everyone to reaffirm their grips.

"Alright, Alright. (To herself), this is bad…" She took a deep breath, looked at Sam, and then at the others.

"So, as you can tell, all of us aren't actually "criminals". We aren't working for these bastards. We are part of a … uhhh…an undercover group plotting against the NOVA. For the past year and a half, we've got loads of pairs in multiple facilities all around the world. Canada, England, China, India, Australia, you name it. This site, here in Japan was a hard nut to crack, but we finally jumped the hurdle two months ago. Now…"

Sam interrupted, "Wait, Rachael. That's enough from our side." He had the calmest voice. It felt as though he said everything (which was not much) respectfully.

All of this was mind-boggling to Eddie, Ollie, and Cain. What were the chances of this happening?

Eddie finally spoke, "Alright that's fair. Looking at the nature of your half-truth, I'll follow. We too work undercover. Freelance, you could say."

Both Rachael and Sam smiled, acknowledging Eddie's level of intellect.

He continued, "We have been following NOVA for almost a year now. We are here to outright pull them out of their roots, BURN THEM, SAVE THEM, ROTTING IN THE DEPTHS OF HELL…"

"Calm down Eddie," Cain interrupted an emotional and furious Eddie. "You see, we lost two of our best friends while fighting. So, it is serving time for NOVA. If you plan to work with us, it would be fueling to both our plans, otherwise, there is always the fun way."

"Yo,"said Rachael, "We have no intention to fight as long as you guys are speaking the truth. We're just here to deliver our duty and any trustworthy help will be accepted."

"Wait. Trust goes both ways. Even if you trust us, I don't. Not after what happened before. If you guys are truly what you show yourselves to be, then prove it. Otherwise, I will be happy to walk the other way…or…if need be, I'll be glad to have you on the other side of my gun." This stirred up the memories of Ray and George inside Eddie which were still fresh cuts on his heart.

Sam replied, "Look Xavier (the three had changed their names for the mission, obviously), we place our trust in you guys. Both he and Rachael nodded for confirmation. "But, we have no obligation to make you trust us. If you want to test us, go ahead. No one's stopping you. We will go on with our mission as we would've, if we never met you. Whether you want to join hands, whether you want to part ways or just to go in alone, is entirely up to you."

These words, although pretty straightforward for Ollie and Cain, weighed on Eddie. It was exactly how Ray would have replied. Memories of Ray flooded into his soul, which fuelled his already high anger.

"Fine. Let's see what happens next."

Everybody was quiet. Nobody spoke anything. No one went to sleep. They all were sitting there steering at each other's faces. Eddie was the only one who retired to his room, but he couldn't sleep either. His fit earlier opened another part of the floodgate he was struggling to patch up.

This gig went on until the wake-up 'screech' at 4:30.

Everybody sitting there was a bit calmer now.

Ollie chose to break the ice, "I don't think anything is gonna work out this way. I think given the evidence found and our passion, we should be able to trust each other. I certainly do."

Rachael interrupted, "What about Mr. Long hair, big ego here."

"Let's give Xavier sometime. The thing is, as we told you about the two friends we lost, one of them was with him since birth. They came a long way. Both were abandoned orphans found by someone at the same place and they grew up together with abond stronger than brothers. He is still in deep regret because he was backstabbedby our old captain."

"Alright, if you say so. Let's give it a try," said Sam.

He seemed to be uneasy after hearing their story. Was it just uneasiness?

In a more serious tone, Cain said, "So, let's try and come clean to each other right."

Everybody nodded. "So, we guys are actually from the US army."

Rachael and Sam were shocked but they might have been expecting this, given the three's intellectual prowess.

"I respect your decision here. But we cannot disclose the exact details ofwhere we are. Just know this much. We too are affiliated with this army", explained Rachael. "There is not much time to go into further details. We have a healthy-sized unit ready to attack the facility on our signal."

Cain replied, "Hmm. Alright, let's talk about the specifics later. We too have a unit backing us, hopefully. But the main problem is there is no way for us to signal them. We are counting on discovering some kind of connection to the surface. But this place is in a world of its own, completely secluded from the 'normal' world. The only ways in and out arethrough the pod-lines which obviously, is unusable for invading, especially with a large number."

"Except, it's not," said Sam. "What do you think we were doing the past month and a half? This place is full of mysteries, probably even for the ones working here. And this place is olllddd… I say this because while meddling around the ventilation system, I stumbled upon a loose tile on the wall. I took it off to reveal a moldy bricked wall beneath. When I touched the bricks they felt loose, so I tried pulling them out. It worked. The whole thing was justcoming apart. I tested the surrounding pieces of the tile and blow my mind to pieces, a large enough space, fit for an adult to pass through opened up before me."

"What?" both Cain and Ollie were shocked.

Sam continued, "On taking apart a few more bricks, what I saw is still surreal."

"Don't tell me… oh my god," you could feel the excitement on Ollie's face as he spoke.

"Yeah…Yeah… There standing in all its beauty was a cave. It looked ancient. Wasn't bricked, just stone chiseled away and wet mud. I quickly loosely fitted the tiles behind me and went to discover its depth. After walking and at places, climbing for a good couple of kilometers, I exited into the back of a closed-down grocery shop, outside the facility.

"I can't believe it. Oh my God!" said Cain.

"It is true though. And, wait for it... There is another one."

"NO FRICKING WAY," Ollie was almost jumping.

"This one is a bigger, still untiled, still wet sand but it leads to a shut-down hospital."

"But that's it. That's what we need. There is away for army units to enter. Good job man." Even Cain was bubbling. "That was quite easy and eventful, innit?"

Then Eddie came out. It was 5 o'clock. Ollie and Cain filled him in on their chat.

He turned to Sam and Rachael, "If what you are saying is true, I'll be happy to join hands. Hear this, I do not have any personal grudge towards but don't you dare to try any funny business."

"See, you're not so bad when you try," said Rachael jokingly.

Everybody laughed including Eddie, as they set out to work.

Skip past to midnight, and they are all sitting in the common room. A tense air flows through the place, as they plan their attack.

After a long discussion, Rachael steps up and says, "Alright boys. So, to sum it all up, the two caves that we know are situated almost opposite each other. So… in four days, both our units are to enter from there, wreak havoc and kick their goddamn asses. Yeah!"

"Yeah, that seems about right," cheered Ollie.

She continued, "So, tomorrow, Eddie is going to enter the smaller cave to go out and transmit both the signals to both the units."

Eddie nodded.

"This just leaves to steer clear of any guards while he is in pursuit."

Cain stated, "Well the tan's probably don't give a damn of what's happening around them. It's only the 'blue' and especially the 'black' ones."

"You don't have to worry about those 'Men in Black'. They won't come there. The place is ancient. No air con, reeking of dead rodents. That's the last place they'd wanna come to," said Sam.

"Well then, let's gear up and get this bread, boys." Eddie's past self was starting to re-emerge. He must've felt better talking to Sam and Rachael.

The next day, everything went smoothly. Eddie did not encounter a single soul of a blue or a black. He successfully transmitted both signals and received confirmation.

He came back and put the plates on the wall which was now devoid of any bricks behind it. You could just stumble upon it and it would fall apart.

All five eagerly waited for the next three days, strategizing their positions and roles. Everyone was pumped up.

Three days passed in the blink of an eye.

On the night before the attack, owing to the advanced nanotech prevalent among the army, they were each equipped with two weapons.

One being their preferred weapon, and a backup compact machine pistol. Both Eddie and Sam had different assault rifles, Ollie had a drumgun like SMG, and Cain went for a thermite sniper rifle. But the most intriguing and sick weapon was Rachael's, who had a long blade, which looked like it was straight out of 'Cyberpunk'. It was huge, with neon purple and green running through it. All the weapons they had were super futuristic and packed some heavy punches. Just know this much, these beasts and shredders.

The weapons were retracted into pieces of each one's clothing and were ready to spring into action with a patterned touch.

As they set out for a "normal" day of work, they split into groups of two, and 3, with Eddie and Sam going towards the larger cave which opened at the hospital, and the other 3 to the smaller one. They were all in the zone and pumped up to fight whoever came in their way.

The army was to strike at around nine when breakfast was just about to end. People would be more carefree at that time. Realistically, nobody would expect any kind of attack in here. But this way would cause the most chaos and confusion due to everyone being cramped up in the cafeteria.

After four unending hours of work, it was finally time. Eddie and Sam were in cafeteria 'A' which was very close to the "cave-cavity", and Rachael, Ollie, and Cain were in cafeteriaB which was on the first floor near the other hole.

Among the prevalent chaos of breakfast, chasing plates, noisy eating, loud talking, and shouting, there was a loud thud. Two parts of the facility just blew up. There was a deathly silence for a moment which was accompanied by a thunderstorm.

The army had entered, rifles in hand, shooting everyone in sight with only oneorder in mind.

"DON'T SHOOT RED."

This was a part of the cryptic sent by Eddie. The five that day dripped up in bright red clothes in contrast to the blue they had to wear everyday while on site. Luckily, they hadn't encountered any "black" that day, who could have spilledmud all over their cake just before it reached its destination.

Part of the plan was for Eddie and Sam to split up in the chaos that followed the army's invasion and eat away the number of people.

Just before parting, Eddie stopped Sam, and said, "Hey! I'm sorry for my rash, distant and untrusting behavior before. The truth is, you and Rachael seem to be very nice people. You remind me of Ray a little bit, I don't know why. Let's keep in touch and work together."

Sam laughed, "Eddie, dude. Trust your instincts. Make it through today for the biggest surprise of your life." As he said this, Sam vanished into the crowd, leaving a dumbfounded Eddie there.

What just happened? What did Sam mean? What could the surprise possibly be?

Eddie had all types of questions spring in his head. But he had no time to ponder over them.

He tapped his watch thrice and formed his sweet A.R and unloaded it in the cafeteria. With everyone in place, raining down hell, it was truly a massacre. The army, while chopping down on people wasinstalling remote explosives all over the place, to detonate after evacuations. Besides these, there were smaller planned explosions all over the place taking out even more confused workers and the armed opposition.

In a matter of 45 minutes, the place was almost empty. With more numbers of the enemy approaching through the pods, the army started its retreat, through the place of their entry, which was now decorated with a shit load of explosives to cause it to collapse.

They started moving out with the fivebehind them providing cover fire along with retreating themselves.

Halfway back through the tunnels, the remote explosives inside the factory were detonated. The sound of the bullets instantly stopped as the air was filled with vibrations from the mind-numbing explosion. Everyone, even at the other end of the tunnels got chills down their spine as they felt the pressure of the blast and the shocks of debris collapsing behind them.

They did it. The whole place was brought down. Everyone re-joined as they emerged out of the tunnels.

But, as they stood there, they heard a huge rumble followed by an unbelievably loud thud. To their horror, the ground where the "facility" one stood saved in taking down with it, the surrounding area in its entirety.

The situation was getting too big. In light of possible Japanese government involvement, they thought it best to get out of there as soon as possible, but only after they had confirmed the final piece of the puzzle, whichwas the mission was put into place.

The army units along with the five headed back to an airport. They were to fly from a private runway.

"Aren't those owned by the government? What's happening here? Ollie was confused.

The head of the unit informed them "Yes, sir. The place we're headed to is government authorized. Apparently, due to a situation that came to light recently, the NOVA group hasbeen recognized internationally as a top-priority test. So, the government of Japan was secretly made aware of your mission and thus authorized this escape."

In the plane-

"Seriously? We were literally shunted out by that pea-brained Bradly before and now when they realized they screwed up…Honestly," said Ollie.

"Dude, forget about it," said Rachael.

"What's the status of phase shiny?"

He replied jokingly, "Oh my God! Drop that name, right now. Anyway, I thought Sam went to confirm."

Just then Sam enters, "Alright, guys I've got good news."

CHAPTER 6

I had just opened my eyes. I felt like my body was on fire. Everything hurt so badly. The restraints on my body made it much worse. I wanted to end it all. But, curse my luck, even that was out of my reach.

I wanted to scream so much that it would tear my body, but I didn't have the slightest bit of energy.

I heard a thud.

"Hee-heehee-hee."

Oh no! It was him. That maniac. The devil incarnate. Please! Please… Help me, somebody.

He didn't say a word just kept laughing. He came closer, leaned over me looked me close in the eyes. It was the first time I had seen him up close.

I couldn't see his entire face but I stared deep into his eyes. They were colorless. Pitch black darkness extending into an endless abyss. I felt like I was falling down that void. No, I was already falling.

I suddenly jolted out as I felt something prick me. Everything suddenly felt a lot clearer. It was raining outside. I could smell the rainwater. The man probably injected me with something.

"Heyy, dude. Story time. Gotta be pumped up for story time, don't weeee?"

The planes had landed back in the USA. They had just landed a huge dub over NOVA.

"Hey, Baldy. Shiny today, aren't we?" said Rachael while laughing.

Yup! This was her phase shiny. The army had managed to capture the bald guy who had previously threatened Rachael and belonged to the black lanes. The bald dude with a shiny head!

He sat there in the interrogation room of an army facility.

Sam, Ollie, Cain, and Rachael, were there. Eddie wasn't. He hadn't metwith them after the attack. They had just gotten the message that he'll be joining them soon and to proceed without him.

Cain went up to the guy, held his chin, and gave him a good smack on the face, "You bastards. What are you lot trying to do? What is this NOVA? What do you guys want? Spill it all out." He punched him again.

The bald dude started laughing.

"What's so funny, huh?'

"You guys. You'll not get it. You all are just kids. Brats in front of NOVA. And I'm afraid the kids have taken up a lot more than they can chew. You wanna know everything. I'll tell you everything. Every single damn thing. But know this, you'll still be HELPLESS and at the end of the way you'll be lying in the middle of nowhere with more holes in your body than you can count."

Cain was not having it. He landed multiple punches on his face. "Just get to the point and tell us about NOVA."

"Angry little boy. Listen now. The NOVA group is more than just a gang of your everyday terrorist with a pipe dream of world domination or with a passion to make something "right". No, no, no, no…NOVA is as large as a country, maybe even more. You can't comprehend what it packs with itself…So, tell me, what do you think NOVA means, as in the name'…Let me spare you the time because you seem to be low on it. NOVA is made up of four letters, N, O, V and, you guessed it, A. Each letter stands for one ofthe generations of owners. Yeah, generations. You already know Mr. O, don't you? Each one of the generals is ruthless. More dangerous than the other. And they do not give one shit about anything. They just want to destroy. And they will come after you for what you did in Tokyo. Ohh…You're gonna pay. Hahaha…"

His evil laughter again. He was enjoying it.

Rachael who was furious now gave him a good beating. She unsheathed her blade from her watch and smacked him in the gut with its neon hilt.

"Cut the crap, Baldy. What do they want? Why are they doing this, and since when?"

He coughed up a little blood and started laughing again. "Oh, you have no idea how long we have operated and dominated the underground scene. We were there even during the Second World War when the French exploded an atomic bomb in 1960. When the Chinese blasted a hydrogen bomb. We were there for it all."

Everyone present in the room staredin disbelief. The unprecedented scale of what he just said shook them from their core. An organization this huge, present in society for almost a century.

"The generals just want one thing and one thing only, DESTRUCTION. Hahahahaha... We've all been waiting... waiting so long. It's finally time now. Hahaha..."

"For what? What are you trying to do?" said Cain as he grabbed him by his t-shirt.

"BOOM...The whole world will come down. At the same time...BOOM. Hahaha..."

Cain, now over his limit, punched him so hard, that he knocked the guy unconscious.

What followed next was pure silence. Nobody had anything to say. They were too shaken to even move.

Just then, Eddie walked in upon an unconscious, beat-up bald dude tied to a chair and 7-8 dumbfounded and expressionless individuals.

He looked like he was in agony.

Without saying a word, he walked up to Sam and stood there for a moment.

And suddenly, out of the blue swung a right hook towards him. Some tried to dodge it, but Eddie was too fast. He ate it with full force.

Without saying anything, with not even a wrinkle on his face, Sam struck back. Eddie just stood there and took the punch.

"What is wrong with you both?" Rachael jumped to stop the sudden outbreak.

"Stay back. Nobody comes close. Don't try to stop us," Eddie shouted as we went for SAM again, this time facing a fist himself.

They both started punching each other mindlessly. Nobody knew what was going on. Everybody stood there in disbelief.

As they fought, owing to Eddie's training regiment, he gained an upper hand.

He got above a knocked down Sam and started punching him in the face.

Suddenly he burst into tears, "Why? Why? Why? Tell me Ray."

"Oi, Eddie. He is not Ray, dude. It's Sam…," Ollie realized what he had said.

As if there wasn't enough silence already. Eddie stopped punching. Sam (or Ray supposedly) stopped as well. Ollie and Cain fell to their knees, Rachael stole her eye contact and looked away.

Both Ollie and Cain were in tears, along with Eddie. Sam/Ray stood up and stayed there with a sad look on his face.

"What are you saying, Eddie? That's not possible…is it? You saw that "O" push him down… with your own eyes, didn't you? See, this is Sam. He is just Sam, he doesn't… even look like Ray." Ollie didn't want to believe it. "It's not true… Tell him… Tell him Sam. Tell him it's you."

Sam kept his silence. He just looked downwards and away from everyone.

Cain asked him, "Why aren't you saying anything? Come on…"

Eddie, who had now stopped crying and was just plain furious. "He won't say anything." (To Ray/Sam) "Why'd you do it, Ray? TELL ME WHY?"

After a few seconds of silence, Ray/Sam finally spoke up. "It's true. I am not Sam." He reached out to his neck and pulled it up to reveal a mask. It was the same face-changing mask that Eddie and the others had used while entering the Tokyo facility.

There he was standing in all his "glory", Ray. "I'm sorry guys." He burst into tears. "I'm s… sorry. I'm back now. I'm back. Eddie, Ollie, Cain." He gave out a huge smile amidst all the tears. Ollie and Cain ran up to him and hugged their 'bro'.

"We missed you dude."

"We really did."

"Me too, guys. Every single day I spent with you for the last few weeks ate me from within, when I was so close to you all but I couldn't do anything."

"Why couldn't you? Why couldn't you do anything? Why hide if you knew it was us?" Eddie seemed to still be angry.

"Because of this right here. I knew it would've caught you all off-guard and a scene like this would have developed. Plus, Rachael and I were under strict orders to uphold my secret as in NOVA's eyes I am dead. I'm so sorry, man. I can understand your pain. Every second I kept you lot in the dark, I rotted from inside. Please, forgive me."

Eddie stood there for a moment, looked up, closed his eyes, and took a deep breath. A tear or two could be seen tricking through the corners of his eyes. He then walked up to Ray and clutched him for a good long hug. Nobody said a word until all four of them started laughing.

They were back normal. Eddie, Ollie, and Cain got 1 of their friends back.

The bald guy was still out cold. Now in the room were just Eddie, Ray, Ollie, Cain, and Rachael.

"So, if you don't mind me asking, Ray. What happened that day at the Grand Canyon," asked Cain. Eddie's and Ollie's eagerness also rise.

Ray responded, "Well, I was unconscious the whole time…"

He took a deep sigh and then continued, "When I fell off… when Mr. O threw me off the Grand Canyon. I probably fell into the Colorado River. And as luck has it, I somehow didn't get decapitated. As I said before I was completely out of it. When I came to my senses. I was in a rundown cell, hung from the ceiling through my arms which were chained above. It must have been around a week. I had zero energy in me… Unable to move. After a few hours of hanging there mindlessly, as the chains felt tighter and tighter, my hunger became deadlier and deadlier, two people entered the cell. The place was pitch black except for a sole light bulb above my head. Those two approached me and without uttering a word came at me with some kind of whip…or…or something. I was already weak. I didn't have the energy to scream. I…I passed out after a couple of minutes. This happened every day. Every day, the five minutes for which I could keep my consciousness, sometimes felt like five years, sometimes flew past in five seconds. The wish to end it all often wandered in my mind. But I couldn't fulfill that either…

They…they must've wanted to keep me alive. I started getting fed a meal a day and a few glasses of water…"

"Let me take it from here," Rachael, who hadn't uttered a word all this time cut in.

"So, you knew about this whole façade?"asked Cain.

"Of course, I knew…well, anyway, turns out the people who got Ray were contracted by NOVA to confirm his and George's kill and to slowly torture them if otherwise."

"What? Talk about being overly cautious," said Ollie.

"So, they found Ray, washed up at the bank of the Colorado River not very far away from the site. They took him in and did what they were told. Now, the unit which I lead and which Ray is a part of now is a branch of the US army unknown to anyone except the top brass. Not even other army personnel…I don't know why I just told you that…"

Everybody was confused, and Ray sighed.

"Well, I guess… It's okay, given everything that's happened. Anyway, we were tasked to conduct an investigation. In the aftermath of the battle and look for any clues. We had been after NOVA fora long time, and this was kept hidden from the rest of the army to maintain secrecy. So, turns out this particular gang was just a lowly bunch of thugs. This is somewhere, NOVA somehow slacked off. They had set up their camp in a cave system inside the Canyon itself and left out tons of evidence all around the place. Used cigarettes, footsteps, bits of food. We eventually found them and discovered about Ray and another guy…his name was I believe…"

"It was Brett," said Ray.

"Yayaya…Brett. So, my unit and I attacked their base late at night. Honestly, they were complete amateurs. No biggie at all… We took in Ray. He was quite crucial at the moment. Unfortunately, we were too late for Brett. He had already given in. To throw dust in NOVA's eyes, we set a mini-explosive to a couple of gas tanks they had in there. The whole place was blasted to pieces along with a fake body to replace Ray. We retreated. The NOVA probably think he's long dead now…"

"I want to spit at negligence. Honestly."

Everyone looked around, to see the bald guy, now awake, sitting and with a huge grinon his face. One of pride and superiority.

"Huh, what you mean?" asked an angry Ollie.

"Hahahaha. You are underestimating NOVA. Do you think they don't know what's going on? What you are scheming. Write this down in stone in your brain. You are a hundred years too young to outsmart the four generals. I'll let you in on something. They know everything. That Ray was alive, about the secret army unit that freed Ray. You must have been thinking, you hit jackpot by discovering Japan. Well, guess what, you did not. It was NOVA that led you to it. Nobody can discover our facilities…unless… we want them to.

We knew about the girl and the dead boy when they joined and we knew about the other three when they came to Japan. We deliberately put you together and led you on, to believe everything is going according to your plan. Your discovering the tunnels, nobody being around when you went in them to send our signals, everything was according to our plan. NOVA was always a hundred steps ahead of you. And… I'll tell you one thing. The Generals don't care about one facility. They wanted to play with you, just to have fun."

The day when they were supposed to be enjoying their one victory over NOVA couldn't have turned more disastrous. One explosion over another. They were dumbfounded… shook. All of their struggles were meaningless. They had been just pawns dancing around in the palms of the NOVA.

"Oh, and another thing," the bald guy seemed to be enjoying this, "You guys know Blazer?"

On hearing the name Eddie instantly became red hot, "WHAT ABOUT HIM? WHO IS HE?" He grabbed the guy's shirt.

"Oi…Oi. Calm down, long hairs. Yeez. Well, Blazer is long dead."

Everybody was astounded.

"At least the Blazer you knew. Hahaha… ohh… honestly he is so stupid. Didn't know when to give up. His death was very gruesome. I believe it was Mr. A. Ha…he stood no chance against Mr. A, especially in melee fighting."

They were particularly shakenby this. Blazer, their captain specialized in hand-to-hand combat. He might have been one at the top of the list of all the melee fighters all around the world. To be defeated so easily… They couldn't imagine how powerful Mr. Awas.

"The one who did you in was Zuck. He is the right-hand man of Mr. O. Dude and is a beast as well. Rumour has it, he has one or two body parts modified by machines." He continued to laugh. At the five present there, at the US army at their uselessness.

"And one last thing. Each of the four generals is more powerful than the other. But… Mr. O is the most carefree. He does not think before acting. He enjoys every last second of the destruction. He is a maniac in that sense. And he enjoyed playing with you a lot. He's gonna come for you again with a head-on attack and you will fall."

CHAPTER 7

I had given up now. There was no hope for me. All that was left for me now was the story the man was telling me and my uselessness and feebleness.

"Awake, huh?" The man's voice seemed to be getting higher and higher in pitch from when I first heard it.

How long ago was it? I don't have any idea.

"Do you like our story? I bet it's fun," he began laughing as he drugged me again.

At this point, I had nothing left. I invested myself in the story trying to find who I was or who he was.

It had been a few hours since the chat with the bald guy.

He couldn't have been left alive. Now, they had a glimpse of the pure terror that the NOVA brought with it. It would be too reckless to even let a grain slip out. The five of them gathered with the army generals for a short-notice meeting.

"This Mr. O guy is going to make his move soon. We gotta do something," Ray said.

"How fast are we talking?"one of the generals asked.

"Based on what that bald guy said, we might have at best three days, four if we're lucky," said Ollie.

"That's too less. We…we can't do much that quickly. At the least, we won't be able to involve any other nation. The complications will take too much time."

"Let's not waste a second then. Start the talks with any possible allied nations right this moment. If they can come then bingo, otherwise we could be standing where we are now," said Eddie.

"You're right, kid," said one of the generals. He immediately made a few calls. "The negotiations are on the move."

"How much manpower can we gather?" asked Cain.

"Ouch. Somewhere around 50,000. Maybe even 75."

"Hmm, try to push the number. I think they would be bringing no less than 150,000," said Ray.

"These bastards," said Eddie. "They wanna come and fight. Let's take the fight to them. General, what's the status with Project Percy?"

"Project Percy, huh? It is still not tested enough for its durability, but it should be functional. Do you wanna risk it?"

"This is going to be an all-out war. I don't care about some tests. We get that thing up and running, we definitely would gain an upper hand," Eddie's pure hatred and anger were evident.

"Get the head engineer on the line, now," the general ordered one of his assistants.

For the next hour or so, through intense discussions, arguments and suggestions, they were sitting upright with a plan in their heads and wills in their hearts. Only one thing mattered in the world right now. CRUSHING NOVA.

The next three days passed in a jiffy, as prepping for the attack took place.

"Welcome to Project Percy," the general announced, as they entered the biggest castle they had ever seen. In the middle of nowhere, with and stretching till the horizon, it was a monolith among monoliths.

"This is Percy standing at whooping 150m, this bad boy is taller than the London Eye. This thing here is fully functioned through AI and equipped with THE BEST defense mechanisms. Anyone enters in a 75m radius on all its sides and Bam! It activated the 100 artillery units and the 250 rifle units present inside it all along its walls." The general was jumping with excitement. "It is equipped with everything you would ever need. Missiles, rocket launcher, observation-control rooms, a stacked among with every kind of weapon… if there's anything I am worried about is its functioning at this stage."

"I can't wait to kick their asses," said Ollie.

Ray stated, "We don't have time to worry about the functioning right now. Without Percy, we would have a confirmed loss anyway. Let's just hope for the best and put everything on the line, General."

All preparations were done. Around 80,000 soldiers were equipped with weapons and stationed all over the fortress that was Percy. Rocket launchers and canons were loaded and kept on standee. Along with all of this, four helicopters were readied up.

Now the ball was in Mr. O's court. And they didn't have to wait long. Within a day, the army got a message stating the movement of an unbelievably large group in the desert towards Percy.

This was it. It was time for the showdown.

Eddie, Ray, Ollie, Cain, and Rachael were dying to go into action. They were all fired up. Everyone from the army was.

The army was held back in only part of their plan. No negotiations with any country were successful.

Everywhere, they were put on hold. But this didn't stop them.

Two hours after they had received the transmission, they spotted the march coming toward them. The horde kept coming closer with more soldiers continuing to emerge from the horizon. Their numbers were so huge, it was unbelievable.

"At least 250,000 people are coming towards us right now," said Ollie who was in charge of satellite imaging and comms.

As soon as the 75m radius was breached, Percy was activated and started shredding the front lives. They shot back in return, but it was no use in front of the superior firepower of Percy's machine guns.

The battle had started.

Canons were shot from both sides. While the NOVA army sustained heavy damage, Percy held up just fine, thanks to his advanced engineering build.

Due to such rapidfire by Percy, the army wasn't able to advance much further. The front few rows were already destroyed.

"They have no natural cover. But they are just blindly moving forward. Blindly, towards death. Why? It's almost like they are just robots." Rachael was surprised by what she was seeing.

But eventually, the army started spreading in all directions. This was a game-changing move. Due to slight imperfections with Percy's system, the nonstop bullets from the NOVA army eventually busted a few of Percy's guns. This made pathways for bits of the army to advance.

Streams of the combatants started leaking towards the fortress. But Percy still had a move up his sleeve. As the army reached closer, its second line of defense, the SMGs were activated. Although slowing them down, the same thing was happening.

"There are too many of them. I don't believe this. The estimated number is way beyond 250,000 now," said Ollie.

"What are we saying?" asked Eddie, who was furious due to the orders of staying inside until the opposition's number dropped now enough.

"It crossed 500,000, and more keep on coming." Tensions in the control room were sky high.

The army had now started popping out compressible nanotech walls and other structures for cover. In places, without these, people were picking up and using their fallen comrades as human shields. The US army was slowly getting cornered.

To put the frosting on top, one of the ten big boi machine guns, the ones installedat the very top and with the most firepower and range suddenly broke down.

Ollie managed to increase the area of his scan and spotted 10 heat signatures around 200 meters from where they were.

"Snipers. Ten. About 200 meters. Northeast," he said.

This was Cain's calling. Those machine guns were crucial. They couldn't afford to lose another one.

He climbed to the top of Percy and confirmed the direction through which the snipers came through.

He set up his thermite power sniper and zoomed in the direction. He spotted the first one pretty quickly. And boom! Right on target.

Without wasting any second, he loaded up the second shot, and boom! He wiped out the tenpeople faster than spreading butter on a toast.

On the other hand, Ollie, who was able to get a scan of a larger radius said, "Guys, you have to see these 200 meters out, and the horde does not end. Out there, they are just rushing in without a second thought. And to have around 700,000 men. I don't know if Percy can hold on much longer."

That was definitely proving itself to be more and more inevitable with one of the large guns gone, the speed of the army ascent was faster than ever.

The General of the Army ordered the helis to move out.

It was time for phase two. All helicopters were sky high, each equipped with one machine gunner and a rocket launcher. The army suffered major damage from this one. Slowly shredding away large areas, the helicopters soared above the hoard. Scrambling here and there, due to their extensive numbers, the blast radius of the rockets was particularly rewarding.

But this didn't go on for long. This plan had an obvious flaw, which couldn't have been anticipated before, given the size of the army that showed up.

If anything, the helis attracted attention. It took less than an instant after the shooting started. And puff, they were gone. But… there was an unseen plus point here. All of the choppers fell over the NOVA army and exploded, taking down with them a lot of people.

"Ollie, the new estimate for the numbers," asked an impatient Eddie.

"Yeah, just a second, it's processing…Alright…Oh my God! I can finally see the end. So, as of now, there are still around 500,000 soldiers out there. That being said, this is around half of the initial number which is maddening in every sense."

Another soldier, working on recon added, "Sir, we got to do something though. And fast. A lot of the guns have been shot down. I don't think the place would hold much longer."

"Hmm, this is a big problem. General, what's the status with phase 3?" asked Ray.

The General replied, "The package should be arriving any minute now."

After a few minutes of impatience and anxiety, one guy suddenly said, "Contact. We have contact. East wall. They have established direct contact with the walls."

"We have to hurry with phase three, General. Percy can't hold up much longer if things stay as they are," stated Ray.

"Any second now."

After a few seconds, a transmission was received, "This is TD-05. Confirming position. Proceeding to target ETA for completion in ten seconds."

This sparked a pinch of joy across the control room. Here it was. Phase three. An army bomber.

As it soared above the army, it dropped two large shells over it. One towards the front and one at the rear end.

This was a big fish. It was one of the most devastating attacks from the army until now. Even the unwavering NOVA army was shaken as panic set in. their formation broke in quite a lot of places, causing confusion and stampedes aided by the piling bodies.

Eddie took hold of the communication mic and shouted, "Percy to TD-05. Turn your course towards the army. Try to fly in low, from the side, and release the aircraft on them. Try to deploy as soon as possible."

"… Copy that, sir." They both knew he wasn't returning. The moment he jumps, he'll be split into a million pieces. But nevertheless, he turned the massive airplane toward the army and sent it. The pilot didn't even jump out. He committed to his duty until his but moment.

As the aircraft received thousands and thousands of bullets it swept a large chunk of the army. The American army clearly had the upper hand.

"I was wondering, Sir General. How come this bomber is the size of an aircraft carrier?" asked Ollie.

"Well, that's the fun part, isn't it?" the General said excitedly. "Open her up (into the microphone)."

The walls and the wings of the bomb fell apart and revealed behind them a dozen army tanks.

"Oooh. What?" laughed Rachael, and so did everybody.

The tanks started chopping the NOVA army from within their ranks. Stomping on whoever came infront of them. Now, these were advanced new-age tanks. Equipped with a long explosive canon at its front and two machine guns sticking out from both sides, it dealt major damage. Due to their superior durability, the tanks survived a bit longer.

They eventually fell victim to the NOVA army's rocket launchers. But, adding up everything, NOVA had already suffered extensive damage.

Theirnumbers had been reduced to 200,000 which when compared to their initial count seems magical.

A sense of relief spread through the control room.

"Finally", screamed Eddie, "Time for PHASE 5."

The orders went through and finally, the US army was mobilized.

About 100,000 passionate soldiers were ready to kick ass. The plan was to decrease the numbers of the opposition to at least to make it one for every two. And this was finally achieved.

Underground trapdoors sprouted all over the battlefield with surprise attacks.

The place wasn't barren and empty anymore. In addition to the numerous fallen helicopters, tanks, and debris from the aircraft carriers, hundreds of thousands of bodies provided cover. There was truly everything on the line.

It was already evening. The Sun was low and the wind started to set in, bringing with a lot of flying sand. Visibility was low and rearing was non-existent.

The battle raged on, the Eddie, Ray, Ollie, Cain, and Rachael got ready for their deployment.

They unsheathed their respective weapons and with all kinds of armored uniforms, fell upon the battlefield. The NOVA army was getting eaten away. The defense was a huge success.

The five of them completely shredded the numbers along with the rest of the US army.

It was now almost the end of the day. The Sun was really low, the sky burned red, and sand set in the atmosphere as numbers onboth sides dwindled. The defenses of Percy were stopped for obvious reasons.

Slowly and steadily, the day-long war died down as the last few hundred were left of the NOVA. It had been a couple of hours since the five entered the field. They too were battered. As everyone pushed themselves. For the final stretch, the battle finally ended. The US army came out on top. Eddie, Ray, Ollie, Cain, and Rachael came out on top. Everybody in the control room and the few lefts on the battleground jumped and shouted with happiness. Everyone was overjoyed. This was one huge step toward stopping the NOVA and preventing the potential destruction of the whole world.

Just as the survivors started moving back inside Percy, everybody's comms system screeched. After about ten seconds of high-pitched screeching, a voice heavier than a tank, and rougher than the surface of the moon slowly started speaking.

"What's happening? General? Comms?" Everybody was startled

"Nine… Eight…"

Nobody know what was happening or where the transmission was coming from.

"Seven…six… five."

A wave of panic set in across the army. What was going to happen at the end of the countdown?

"Four…Three…Two…One…Hahahahahaha…" There was heavy laughter.

"Boom."

Everything went numb. Everyone present there crumbled under the sheer volume of what happened next. Everything went poof.

The whole world was set ablaze, as the few hundred survivors of the war lay there, under the darkening sky unaware of the fate that awaited Earth.

CHAPTER 8

I just woke up. I felt like I had been sleeping for ages. The story that the man had been telling me was still fresh in my head.

So, the story brings us here. Hmmm, that explains the gloominess outside, the sadness in the atmosphere. I must have been one of the survivors.

I spent the next few minutes thinking over the whole story, pitying the heroes, envying the NOVA.

I looked around. He was not here. Where could he have gone?

I tried to move, but I was still chained to the bed.

Just then, there was a loud banging on the door. Who was it? There had been nobody besides that man. Could it be…? Could it be someone who came to rescue me? Someone who remembers me? I was overjoyed.

"OPEN THE DOOR," the voice was very loud.

Bang…Bang…Bang…

"OPEN, DAMNIT …OR … I'M BREAKING IN."

Bang…Bang…Bang…

I heard a gun cock. Then multiple guns cocks, this time louder.

Bam! The door burst open, and in came three donny's loaded with guns.

Suddenly a bullet shot from my right side and hit one of the newcomers. They started shooting toward the bullet's origin.

"Aaah…, it was the man's voice. There was a noise of glass breaking. Oh! I didn't realize it, but the man must have been in the room, lurking in a corner. He probably jumped out the window.

The people who had just rushed in came towards me. A gush of excitement came over me.

One of them spoke, "How the hell did you get here?"